THE INDIAN
IN THE CUPBOARD

Lynne Reid Banks was born in London in 1929. Her father was a GP and her mother had been a well-known actress. Aged ten when the Second World War began, she was evacuated to Canada with her mother and cousin, where she spent the war in Saskatoon, a small prairie town. When the family was reunited in 1945 Lynne had to learn secretarial skills before she was allowed to study for the stage. After acting for five years, her father died, and she went over to journalism, eventually becoming one of the first women reporters on British TV in 1955. Seven years later, shortly after the publication of her first novel, she emigrated to Israel where she married and lived throughout the 1960s, teaching, writing and having three sons.

She returned to the UK with her family in 1971 and has lived ever since in London and, more recently, Dorset, writing full-time, travelling and giving talks. She particularly likes going into schools abroad as a volunteer teacher, and has done so in India, Israel, Nepal, Zimbabwe, Tanzania, Navajoland in Arizona, Bulgaria and Hungary.

Collins Modern Classics

The Indian in the Cupboard

by
Lynne Reid Banks

illustrated by
Piers Sanford

Collins

An imprint of HarperCollinsPublishers

For Omri – Who else?

First published in Great Britain by J. M. Dent & Sons Ltd in 1981
First published in paperback by Dragon Books in 1981
First published by Collins in 1988

First published as a Collins Modern Classic in 2000

1 3 5 7 9 8 6 4 2

CollinsChildren'sBooks is a division of HarperCollinsPublishers Ltd,
77-85 Fulham Palace Road, Hammersmith, London W6 8JB

Printed and bound in Great Britain by
Omnia Books Limited, Glasgow

ISBN 0 00 675483 X

CONTENTS

Chapter One

BIRTHDAY PRESENTS

IT WAS NOT that Omri didn't appreciate Patrick's birthday present to him. Far from it. He was really very grateful – sort of. It was, without a doubt, very kind of Patrick to give Omri anything at all, let alone a secondhand plastic Red Indian which he himself had finished with.

The trouble was, though, that Omri was getting a little fed up with small plastic figures, of which he had loads. Biscuit-tinsful, probably three or four if they were all put away at the same time, which they never were because most of the time they were scattered about in the bathroom, the loft, the kitchen, the breakfast-room, not to mention Omri's bedroom and the garden. The compost heap was full of soldiers which, over several autumns, had been raked up with the leaves by Omri's mother, who was rather careless about such things.

Omri and Patrick had spent many hours together playing with their joint collections of plastic toys. But now they'd had about enough of them, at least for the moment, and that was why, when Patrick brought his present to school on Omri's birthday, Omri was disappointed. He tried not to show it, but he was.

"Do you really like him?" asked Patrick as Omri stood silently with the Indian in his hand.

"Yes, he's fantastic," said Omri in only a slightly flattish voice. "I haven't got an Indian."

"I know."

"I haven't got any cowboys either."

"Nor have I. That's why I couldn't play anything with him."

Omri opened his mouth to say, "I won't be able to either," but, thinking that might hurt Patrick's feelings, he said nothing, put the Indian in his pocket and forgot about it.

After school there was a family tea, and all the excitement of his presents from his parents and his two older brothers. He was given his dearest wish – a skateboard complete with kick-board and cryptonic wheels from his mum and dad, and from his eldest brother, Adiel, a helmet. Gillon, his other brother, hadn't bought him anything because he had no money (his pocket-money had been stopped some time ago in connection with a very unfortunate accident involving their father's bicycle). So when Gillon's turn came to give Omri a present, Omri was very surprised when a large parcel was put before him, untidily wrapped in brown paper and string.

"What is it?"

"Have a look. I found it in the alley."

The alley was a narrow passage that ran along the bottom of the garden where the dustbins stood. The three boys used to play there sometimes, and occasionally found treasures that other – perhaps richer – neighbours had thrown away. So Omri was quite excited as he tore off the paper.

Inside was a small white metal cupboard with a mirror in the door, the kind you see over the basin in old-fashioned bathrooms.

You might suppose Omri would once again be disappointed, because the cupboard was fairly plain and, except for a shelf, completely empty, but oddly enough he was very pleased with it. He loved cupboards of any sort because of the fun of keeping things in them. He was not a very tidy boy in general, but he did like arranging things in cupboards and drawers and then opening them later and finding them just as he'd left them.

"I do wish it locked," he said.

"You might say thank you before you start complaining," said Gillon.

"It's got a keyhole," said their mother. "And I've got a whole boxful of keys. Why don't you try the smaller ones and see if any of them fit?"

Most of the keys were much too big, but there were half a dozen that were about the right size. All but one of these were very ordinary. The un-ordinary one was the most interesting key in the whole collection, small with a complicated lock-part and a fancy top. A narrow strip of red satin ribbon was looped through one of its curly openings. Omri saved that key to the last.

None of the others fitted, and at last he picked up the curly-topped key and carefully put it in the keyhole on the cupboard door, just below the knob. He did hope very much that it would turn, and regretted wasting his birthday-cake-cutting wish on something so silly (or rather, unlikely) as that he might pass his spelling test the next day, which it would take real magic to bring about as he hadn't even looked at the words since they'd been given out four days ago. Now he closed his eyes and unwished the test-pass and wished instead that this little twisty key would turn Gillon's present into a secret cupboard.

The key turned smoothly in the lock. The door wouldn't open.

"Hey! Mum! I've found one!"

"Have you, darling? Which one?" His mother came to look. "Oh, *that* one! How very odd. That was the key to my grandmother's jewel-box, that she got from Florence. It was made of red leather and it fell to bits at last, but she kept the key and gave it to me. She was most terribly poor when she died, poor old sweetie, and kept crying because she had nothing to leave me, so in the end I said I'd rather have this little key than all the jewels in the world. I threaded it on that bit of ribbon – it was much longer then – and hung it round my neck and told her I'd always wear it and remember her. And I did for a long time. But then the ribbon broke and I nearly lost it."

"You could have got a chain for it," said Omri.

She looked at him. "You're right," she said. "I should have done just that. But I didn't. And now it's your cupboard key. Please don't lose it, Omri, will you."

Omri put the cupboard on his bedside table, and opening it, looked inside thoughtfully. What would he put in it?

"It's supposed to be for medicines," said Gillon. "You could keep your nose-drops in it."

"No! That's just wasting it. Besides, I haven't any other medicines."

"Why don't you pop this in?" his mother suggested, and

opened her hand. In it was Patrick's Red Indian. "I found it when I was putting your trousers in the washing-machine."

Omri carefully stood the Indian on the shelf.

"Are you going to shut the door?" asked his mother.

"Yes. And lock it."

He did this and then kissed his mother and she turned the light out and he lay down on his side looking at the cupboard. He felt very content. Just as he was dropping off to sleep his eyes snapped open. He had thought he heard a little noise… but no. All was quiet. His eyes closed again.

In the morning there was no doubt about it. The noise actually woke him.

He lay perfectly still in the dawn light staring at the cupboard, from which was now coming a most extraordinary series of sounds. A pattering; a tapping; a scrabbling; and − surely? − a high-pitched noise like − well, almost like a tiny voice.

To be truthful, Omri was petrified. Who wouldn't be? Undoubtedly there was something alive in that cupboard. At last, he put out his hand and touched it. He pulled very carefully, the door was tight shut. But as he pulled the cupboard moved, just slightly. The noise from inside instantly stopped.

He lay still for a long time, wondering. Had he imagined it?

The noise did not start again. At last he cautiously turned the key and opened the cupboard door.

The Indian was gone.

Omri sat up sharply in bed and peered into the dark corners. Suddenly he saw him. But he wasn't on the shelf any more, he was in the bottom of the cupboard. And he wasn't standing upright. He was crouching in the darkest corner, half hidden by the front of the cupboard. And he was alive.

Omri knew that immediately. To begin with, though the Indian was trying to keep perfectly still – as still as Omri had kept, lying in bed a moment ago – he was breathing heavily. His bare, bronze shoulders rose and fell, and were shiny with sweat. The single feather sticking out of the back of his headband quivered, as if the Indian were trembling. And as Omri peered closer, and his breath fell on the tiny huddled figure, he saw it jump to its feet; its minute hand made a sudden, darting movement towards its belt and came to rest clutching the handle of a knife smaller than the shaft of a drawing-pin.

Neither Omri nor the Indian moved for perhaps a minute and a half. They hardly breathed either. They just stared at each other. The Indian's eyes were black and fierce and frightened. His lower lip was drawn down from shining white teeth, so small you could scarcely see them except when they caught the light. He stood pressed against the inside wall of the cupboard, clutching his knife, rigid with terror, but defiant.

The first coherent thought that came into Omri's mind as he began to get over the shock was, "I must call the others!" – meaning his parents and brothers. But something (he wasn't sure what) stopped him. Maybe he was afraid that if he took his eyes off the Indian for even a moment, he would vanish, or become plastic again, and then when the others came running they would all laugh and accuse Omri of making things up. And who could blame anyone for not believing *this* unless they saw it with their own eyes?

Another reason Omri didn't call anyone was that, if he was not dreaming and the Indian had really come alive, it was certainly the most marvellous thing that had ever happened to Omri in his life and he wanted to keep it to himself, at least at first.

His next thought was that he must somehow get the Indian in his hand. He didn't want to frighten him any further, but he *had* to touch him. He simply had to. He reached his hand slowly into the cupboard.

The Indian gave a fantastic leap into the air. His black pigtail flew and the air ballooned out his loose-fitting leggings. His knife, raised above his head, flashed. He gave a shout which, even though it was a tiny shout to match his body, was nevertheless loud enough to make Omri jump. But not so much as he jumped when the little knife pierced his finger deeply enough to draw a drop of blood.

Omri stuck his finger in his mouth and sucked it and thought how gigantic he must look to the tiny Indian and how fantastically brave he had been to stab him. The Indian stood there, his feet, in moccasins, planted apart on the white-painted metal floor, his chest heaving, his knife held ready and his black eyes wild. Omri thought he was magnificent.

"I won't hurt you," he said. "I only want to pick you up."

The Indian opened his mouth and a stream of words, spoken in that loud-tiny voice, came out, not one of which Omri could understand. But he noticed that the Indian's strange grimace never changed – he could speak without closing his lips.

"Don't you speak English?" asked Omri. All the Indians in films spoke a sort of English; it would be terrible if his Indian couldn't. How would they talk to each other?

The Indian lowered his knife a fraction.

"I speak," he grunted.

Omri breathed deeply in relief. "Oh, good! Listen, I don't know how it happened that you came to life, but it must be something to do with this cupboard, or perhaps the key – anyway, here you are, and I think you're great, I don't mind that you stabbed me, only please can I pick you up? After all, you are my Indian," he finished in a very reasonable tone.

He said all this very quickly while the Indian stared at him. The knife-point went down a little further, but he didn't answer.

"Well? Can I? Say something!" urged Omri impatiently.

"I speak *slowly*," grunted the miniature Indian at last.

"Oh." Omri thought, and then said, very slowly, "Let — me — pick — you — up."

The knife came up again in an instant, and the Indian's knees bent into a crouch.

"No."

"Oh, *please*."

"You touch — I kill!" the Indian growled ferociously.

You might have expected Omri to laugh at this absurd threat from a tiny creature scarcely bigger than his middle finger, armed with only a pin-point. But Omri didn't laugh. He didn't even feel like laughing. This Indian — *his* Indian — was behaving in every way like a real live Red Indian brave, and despite the vast difference in their sizes and strengths, Omri respected him and even, odd as it sounds, feared him at that moment.

"Oh, okay, I won't then. But there's no need to get angry. I don't want to hurt you." Then, as the Indian looked baffled, he said, in what he supposed was Indian-English, "Me – no – hurt – you."

"You come near, I hurt *you*," said the Indian swiftly.

Omri had been half lying in bed all this time. Now, cautiously and slowly, he got up. His heart was thundering in his chest. He couldn't be sure why he was being cautious. Was it so as not to frighten the Indian, or because he was frightened himself? He wished one of his brothers would come in, or better still, his father… But no one came.

Standing in his bare feet he took the cupboard by its top corners and turned it till it faced the window. He did this very carefully but nevertheless the Indian was jolted, and, having nothing to hold on to, he fell down. But he was on his feet again in a second, and he had not let go of his knife.

"Sorry," said Omri.

The Indian responded with a noise like a snarl.

There was no more conversation for the next few minutes. Omri looked at the Indian in the early sunlight. He was a splendid sight. He was about seven centimetres tall. His blue-black hair, done in a plait and pressed to his head by a coloured headband, gleamed in the sun. So did the minuscule muscles of his tiny naked torso, and the reddish skin of his arms. His legs were covered with buckskin trousers which had some decoration on them too small to see properly, and his belt was a thick hide thong twisted into a knot in front. Best of all, somehow, were his moccasins. Omri found himself wondering (not for the first time recently) where his magnifying glass was. It was the only way he would ever be able to see and appreciate the intricate embroidery, or beadwork, or whatever it was which encrusted the Indian's shoes and clothes.

Omri looked as closely as he dared at the Indian's face. He expected to see paint on it, war-paint, but there was none. The turkey-feather which had been stuck in the headband had come out when the Indian fell and was now lying on the floor of the cupboard. It was about as big as the spike on a conker, but it was a real feather. Omri suddenly asked:

"Were you always this small?"

"I no small! You, big!" the Indian shouted angrily.

"No——" began Omri, but then he stopped.

He heard his mother beginning to move about next door. The Indian heard it too. He froze. The door of the next room opened. Omri knew that at any moment his mother would come in to wake him for school. In a flash he had bent down and whispered, "Don't worry! I'll be back." And he closed and locked the cupboard door and jumped back into bed.

"Come on, Omri. Time to get up."

She bent down and kissed him, paying no attention to the cupboard, and went out again, leaving the door wide open.

Chapter Two

THE DOOR IS SHUT

OMRI GOT DRESSED in a state of such high excitement that he could scarcely control his fumbling fingers enough to do up buttons and tie his shoe-laces. He'd thought he was excited yesterday, on his birthday, but it was nothing compared to how he felt now.

He was dying to open the cupboard door and have another look, but the landing outside his bedroom door was like a railway station at this hour of the morning — parents and brothers passing continually, and if he were to close his door for a moment's privacy somebody would be sure to burst in. He'd nip up after breakfast and have a quick look when he was supposed to be cleaning his teeth...

However, it didn't work out. There was a stupid row at

the breakfast table because Adiel took the last of the Rice Krispies, and although there were plenty of cornflakes, not to mention Weetabix, the other two fairly set upon Adiel and made such an awful fuss that their mother lost her temper, and the end of it was nobody got to clean their teeth at all.

They were all bundled out of the house at the last minute — Omri even forgot to take his swimming things although it was Thursday, the day his class went to the pool. He was an excellent swimmer and he was so annoyed when he remembered (halfway to school, too late to go back) that he turned on Adiel and shouted, "You made me forget my swimming stuff!" and bashed him. That naturally led to them all being late for school, and furthermore, arriving in a very grubby condition.

All this actually pushed the Indian right out of Omri's mind. But the minute he set eyes on Patrick, he remembered. And not for one single second for the rest of the day was that Indian out of Omri's thoughts.

You may imagine the temptation to tell Patrick what had happened. Several times Omri very nearly did tell him, and he couldn't help dropping a number of tantalizing hints.

"Your present was the best thing I got."

Patrick looked rather astonished. "I thought you got a skateboard!"

"Ye-es... But I like yours better."

"Better than a skateboard? Are you having me on?"

"Yours turned out to be more exciting."

Patrick just stared at him. "Are you being sarcastic?"

"No."

Later, after they'd had the spelling test and Omri had been marked three right out of ten, Patrick joked, "I bet the plastic Indian could have done better."

Unwarily, Omri replied, "Oh, I don't think he can *write* English, he can only just speak—"

He stopped himself quickly, but Patrick was giving him a very odd look. "What?"

"Nothing."

"No, what did you say about him speaking?"

Omri wrestled with himself. He wanted to keep his secret; in any case Patrick wouldn't believe him. Yet the need to talk about it was very strong. "He can speak," he said slowly at last.

"Beard," said Patrick, which was their school slang for 'I don't believe you.'

Instead of insisting, Omri said nothing more, and that led Patrick to ask, "Why did you say that, about him speaking?"

"He does."

"*Itchy* beard." (Which of course means the same only more so.)

Omri refused to get involved in an argument. He was somehow scared that if he talked about the Indian, something bad would happen. In fact, as the day went on and he longed more and more to get home, he began to feel certain that the whole incredible happening – well, not that it hadn't happened, but that something would go wrong. All his thoughts, all his dreams were centred on the miraculous, endless possibilities opened up by a real, live miniature Indian of his very own. It would be too terrible if the whole thing turned out to be some sort of mistake.

After school Patrick wanted him to stay in the school grounds and skateboard. For weeks Omri had longed to do this, but had never had his own skateboard till now. So it was quite beyond Patrick's understanding when Omri said, "I can't, I have to get home. Anyway, I didn't bring it."

"Why not? Are you crazy? Why do you have to get home, anyway?"

"I want to play with the Indian."

Patrick's eyes narrowed in disbelief. "Can I come?"

Omri hesitated. But no, it wouldn't do. He must get to know the Indian himself before he thought of introducing him to anyone else, even Patrick.

Besides, the most awful thought had come to him during the last lesson which had made it almost impossible

for him to sit still. If the Indian were real, and not just —
well, moving plastic, as Pinocchio had been moving wood,
then he would need food, and other things. And Omri had
left him shut up in the dark all day with nothing. Perhaps
— what if there were not enough air for him in that
cupboard? The door fitted very tight… How much air
would such a very small creature need? What if — what if
the Indian were — what if he'd *died*, shut up there? What if
Omri had killed him?

At the very best, the Indian must have passed a horrible
day in that dark prison. Omri was dismayed at the thought
of it. Why had he allowed himself to be drawn into that silly
row at breakfast instead of slipping away and making sure
the Indian was all right? The mere thought that he might be
dead was frightening Omri sick. He ran all the way home,
burst through the back door, and raced up the stairs without
even saying hello to his mother.

He shut the door of his bedroom and fell on his knees
beside the bedside table. With a hand that shook, he turned
the key in the lock and opened the cupboard door.

The Indian lay there on the floor of the cupboard, stiff
and stark. Too stiff! That was not a dead body. Omri picked
it up. It was an 'it', not a 'he', any more.

The Indian was made of plastic again.

Omri knelt there, appalled — too appalled to move. He

had killed his Indian, or done something awful to him. At the same time he had killed his dream — all the wonderful, exciting, secret games that had filled his imagination all day. But that was not the main horror. His Indian had been real — not a mere toy, but a person. And now here he lay in Omri's hand — cold, stiff, lifeless. Somehow through Omri's own fault.

How had it happened?

It never occurred to Omri now that he had imagined the whole incredible episode this morning. The Indian was in a completely different position from the one he had been in when Patrick gave him to Omri. *Then* he had been standing on one leg, as if doing a war-dance — knees bent, one moccasined foot raised, both elbows bent too and with one fist (with the knife in it) in the air. Now he lay flat, legs apart, arms at his sides. His eyes were closed. The knife was no longer a part of him. It lay separately on the floor of the cupboard.

Omri picked it up. The easiest way to do this, he found, was to wet his finger and press it down on the tiny knife, which stuck to it. It, too, was plastic, and could no more have pierced human skin than a twist of paper. Yet it had pierced Omri's finger this morning — the little mark was still there. But this morning it had been a real knife.

Omri stroked the Indian with his finger. He felt a painful

thickness in the back of his throat. The pain of sadness, disappointment, and a strange sort of guilt, burnt inside him as if he had swallowed a very hot potato which wouldn't cool down. He let the tears come, and just knelt there and cried for about ten minutes.

Then he put the Indian back in the cupboard and locked the door because he couldn't bear to look at him any longer.

That night at supper he couldn't eat anything, and he couldn't talk. His father touched his face and said it felt very hot. His mother took him upstairs and put him to bed and oddly enough he didn't object. He didn't know if he was ill or not, but he felt so bad he was quite glad to be made a fuss of. Not that that improved the basic situation, but it was some comfort.

"What is it, Omri? Tell me," coaxed his mother. She stroked his hair and looked at him tenderly and questioningly, and he nearly told her everything, but then he suddenly rolled over on his face.

"Nothing. Really."

She sighed, kissed him, and left the room, closing the door softly after her.

As soon as she had gone, he heard something. A scratching – a muttering – a definitely *alive* sound. Coming from the cupboard.

Omri snapped his bedside light on and stared wide-eyed at his own face in the mirror on the cupboard door. He stared at the key with its twisted ribbon. He listened to the sounds, now perfectly clear.

Trembling, he turned the key and there was the Indian, on the shelf this time, almost exactly level with Omri's face. Alive again!

Again they stared at each other. Then Omri asked falteringly, "What happened to you?"

"Happen? Good sleep happen. Cold ground. Need blanket. Food. Fire."

Omri gaped. Was the little man giving him orders? Undoubtedly he was! Because he waved his knife, now back in his hand, in an unmistakable way.

Omri was so happy he could scarcely speak.

"Okay – you stay there – I'll get food – don't worry," he gasped as he scrambled out of bed.

He hurried downstairs, excited but thoughtful. What could it all mean? It was puzzling, but he didn't bother worrying about it too much. His main concern was to get downstairs without his parents hearing him, get to the kitchen, find some food that would suit the Indian, and bring it back without anyone asking questions.

Fortunately his parents were in the living-room watching television, so he was able to tiptoe to the kitchen along the dark passage. Once there, he dared not turn on a light; but there was the fridge light and that was enough.

He surveyed the inside of the fridge. What did Indians eat? Meat, chiefly, he supposed — buffalo meat, rabbits, the sort of animals they could shoot on their prairies. Needless to say there was nothing like that.

Biscuits, jam, peanut butter, that kind of thing was no problem, but somehow Omri felt sure these were not Indian foods. Suddenly his searching eyes fell on an open tin of sweetcorn. He found a paper plate in the drawer where the picnic stuff lived, and took a good teaspoon of corn. Then he broke off a crusty corner of bread. Then he thought of some cheese. And what about a drink? Milk? Surely, Indian braves did not drink milk? They usually drank something called 'fire-water' in films, which was presumably a hot drink, and Omri dared not heat anything. Ordinary non-fire water would have to do, unless... What about some Coke? That was an American drink. Luckily there was a bit in a big bottle left over from the birthday party, so he took that. He did wish there were some cold meat, but there just wasn't.

Clutching the Coke bottle by the neck in one hand and the paper plate in the other, Omri sneaked back upstairs with fast-beating heart. All was just as he had left it, except that the Indian was sitting on the edge of the shelf dangling his legs and trying to sharpen his knife on the metal. He jumped up as soon as he saw Omri.

"Food?" he asked eagerly.

"Yes, but I don't know if it's what you like."

"I like. Give, quick!"

But Omri wanted to arrange things a little. He took a pair of scissors and cut a small circle out of the paper plate. On this he put a crumb of bread, another of cheese, and one kernel of the sweetcorn. He handed this offering to the Indian, who backed off, looking at the food with hungry eyes but trying to keep watch on Omri at the same time.

"Not touch! You touch, use knife!" he warned.

"All right, I promise not to. Now you can eat."

Very cautiously the Indian sat down, this time cross-legged on the shelf. At first he tried to eat with his left hand keeping the knife at the ready in his right, but he was so hungry he soon abandoned this effort, laid the knife close at his side and, grabbing the bread in one hand and the little crumb of cheese in the other, he began to tear at them ravenously.

When these two apparently familiar foods had taken the edge off his appetite, he turned his attention to the single kernel of corn.

"What?" he asked suspiciously.

"Corn. Like you have—" Omri hesitated. "Where you come from," he said.

It was a shot in the dark. He didn't know if the Indian 'came from' anywhere, but he meant to find out. The Indian grunted, turning the corn about in both hands, for it was half as big as his head. He smelt it. A great grin spread over his face. He nibbled it. The grin grew wider. But then he held it away and looked again, and the grin vanished.

"Too big," he said. "Like you," he added accusingly.

"Eat it. It's the same stuff."

The Indian took a bite. He still looked very suspicious, but he ate and ate. He couldn't finish it, but he evidently liked it.

"Give meat," he said finally.

"I'm sorry, I can't find any tonight, but I'll get you some tomorrow," said Omri.

After another grunt, the Indian said, "Drink!"

Omri had been waiting for this. From the box where he kept his Action Man things he had brought a plastic mug. It was much too big for the Indian but it was the best he could do. Into it, with extreme care, he now poured a minute amount of Coke from the huge bottle.

He handed it to the Indian, who had to hold it with both hands and still almost dropped it.

"What?" he barked, after smelling it.

"Coca-Cola," said Omri, enthusiastically pouring some for himself into a toothmug.

"Fire-water?"

"No, it's cold. But you'll like it."

The Indian sipped, swallowed, gulped. Gulped again. Grinned.

"Good?" asked Omri.

"Good!" said the Indian.

"Cheers!" said Omri, raising his toothmug as he'd seen his parents do when they were having a drink together.

"What cheers?"

"I don't know!" said Omri, feeling excessively happy, and drank. His Indian — eating and drinking! He *was* real, a real, flesh-and-blood person! It was too marvellous. Omri felt he might die of delight.

"Do you feel better now?" he asked.

"I better. You not better," said the Indian. "You still big. You stop eat. Get right size."

Omri laughed aloud, then stopped himself hastily.

"It's time to sleep," he said.

"Not now. Big light. Sleep when light go."

"I can make the light go," said Omri, and switched out his bedside lamp.

In the darkness came a thin cry of astonishment and fear. Omri switched it on again.

The Indian was now gazing at him with something more than respect — a sort of awe.

"You spirit?" he asked in a whisper.

"No," said Omri. "And this isn't the sun. It's a lamp. Don't you have lamps?"

The Indian peered where he was pointing. "That lamp?" he asked unbelievingly. "Much big lamp. Need much oil."

"But this isn't an oil lamp. It works by electricity."

"Magic?"

"No, electricity. But speaking of magic — how did you get here?"

The Indian looked at him steadily out of his black eyes. "You not know?"

"No, I don't. You were a toy. Then I put you in the cupboard and locked the door. When I opened it, you were real. Then I locked it again, and you went back to being plastic. Then—"

He stopped sharply. Wait! What if — he thought furiously. It was possible! In which case…

"Listen," he said excitedly. "I want you to come out of there. I'll find you a much more comfortable place. You said you were cold. I'll make you a proper tepee—"

"Tepee!" the Indian shouted. "I not live tepee! I live longhouse!"

Omri was so eager to test his theory about the cupboard

that he was impatient. "You'll have to make do with a tepee tonight," he said. Hastily he opened a drawer and took out a biscuit tin full of little plastic people. Somewhere in here was a plastic tepee... "Ah, here!" He pounced on it – a small, pinkish, cone-shaped object with designs rather badly painted on its plastic sides. "Will this do?"

He put it on the shelf beside the Indian, who looked at it with the utmost scorn.

"*This* – tepee?" he said. He touched its plastic side and made a face. He pushed it with both hands – it slid along the shelf. He bent and peered in through the triangular opening. Then he actually spat on the ground, or rather, on the shelf.

"Oh," said Omri, rather crestfallen. "You mean it's not good enough."

"Not want toy," said the Indian, and turned his back, folding both arms across his chest with an air of finality.

Omri saw his chance. With one quick movement he had picked up the Indian by the waist between his thumb and forefinger. In doing this he pinned the knife, which was in the Indian's belt, firmly to his side. The dangling Indian twisted, writhed, kicked, made a number of ferocious and hideous faces – but beyond that he was helpless and he evidently knew it, for after a few moments he decided it was more dignified to stop struggling. Instead, he folded his tiny arms across his chest once again, put his head back, and stared with proud defiance at Omri's face, which was now level with his own.

For Omri, the feeling of holding this little creature in his fingers was very strange and wonderful. If he had had any doubts that the Indian was truly alive, the sensation he had now would have put them to rest. His body was heavier now, warm and firm and full of life — through Omri's thumb, on the Indian's left side, he could feel his heart beating wildly, like a bird's.

Although the Indian felt strong, Omri could sense how fragile he was, how easily an extra squeeze could injure him. He would have liked to feel him all over, his tiny arms and legs, his hair, his ears, almost too small to see — yet when he saw how the Indian, who was altogether in his power, faced him boldly and hid his fear, he lost all desire to handle him; he felt it was cruel, and insulting to the Indian, who was no longer his plaything but a person who had to be respected.

Omri put him down gently on the chest-of-drawers where the cupboard stood. Then he crouched down till his face was again level with the Indian's.

"Sorry I did that," he said.

The Indian, breathing heavily and with his arms still folded, said nothing, but stared haughtily at him, as if nothing he did could affect him in any way.

"What's your name?" asked Omri.

"Little Bull," said the Indian, pointing proudly to himself. "Iroquois brave. Son of Chief. You son of Chief?" he shot at Omri fiercely.

"No," said Omri humbly.

"Hm!" snorted Little Bull with a superior look. "Name?"

Omri told him. "Now we must find you another place to sleep – outside the cupboard. Surely you sleep in tepees sometimes?"

"Never," said Little Bull firmly.

"I've never heard of an Indian who didn't," said Omri with equal firmness. "You'll have to tonight, anyway."

"Not this," said the Indian. "This no good. And fire. I want fire."

"I can't light a real fire in here. But I'll make you a tepee. It won't be very good, but I promise you a better one tomorrow."

He looked round. It was good, he thought, that he never put anything away. Now everything he needed was strewn about the floor and on tables and shelves, ready to hand.

Starting with some pick-up-sticks and a bit of string, he made a sort of cone-shape, tied at the top. Around this he draped, first a handkerchief, and then, when that didn't seem firm enough, a bit of old felt from a hat that had been in the dressing-up crate. It was fawn coloured, fortunately, and looked rather like animal hide. In fact, when it was pinned together at the back with a couple of safety-pins and a slit cut for an entrance, the whole thing looked pretty good, especially with the poles sticking up through a hole in the top.

Omri stood it up carefully on the chest-of-drawers and anxiously awaited Little Bull's verdict. The Indian walked round it four times slowly, went down on hands and knees and crawled in through the flap, came out again after a minute, tugged at the felt, stood back to look at the poles, and finally gave a fairly satisfied grunt. However, he wasn't going to pass it without any criticism at all.

"No pictures," he growled. "If *tepee*, then need pictures."

"I don't know how to do them," said Omri.

"I know. You give colours. I make."

"Tomorrow," said Omri, who, despite himself, was beginning to feel very sleepy.

"Blanket?"

Omri fished out one of the Action Man's sleeping-rolls.

"No good. No keep out wind."

Omri started to object that there was no wind in his bedroom, but then he decided it was easier to cut up a square out of one of his old sweaters, so he did that. It was a red one with a stripe round the bottom and even Little

Bull couldn't hide his approval as he held it up, then wrapped it round himself.

"Good. Warm. I sleep now."

He dropped on his knees and crawled into the tent. After a moment he stuck his head out.

"Tomorrow talk. You give Little Bull meat – fire – paint – much things." He scowled fiercely up at Omri. "Good?"

"Good," said Omri, and indeed nothing in his life had ever seemed so full of promise.

Chapter Three

THIRTY SCALPS

WITHIN A FEW minutes, loud snores – well, not loud, but loud for the Indian – began to come out of the tepee, but Omri, sleepy as he was himself, was not quite ready for bed. He had an experiment to do.

As far as he had figured it out so far, the cupboard, or the key, or both together, brought plastic things to life, *or if they were already alive, turned them into plastic.* There were a lot of questions to be answered, though. Did it only work with plastic? Would, say, wooden or metal figures also come to life if shut up in the cupboard? How long did they have to stay in there for the magic to work? Overnight? Or did it happen straight away?

And another thing – what about objects? The Indian's

clothes, his feather, his knife, all had become real. Was this just because they were part of the original plastic figure? If he put – well, anything you like, the despised plastic tepee for instance, into the cupboard and locked the door, would that be real in the morning? And what would happen to a real object, if he put that in?

He decided to make a double trial.

He stood the plastic Indian tent on the shelf of the cupboard. Beside it he put a Matchbox car. Then he closed the cupboard door. He didn't lock it. He counted slowly to ten.

Then he opened the door.

Nothing had happened.

He closed the door again, and this time locked it with his great-grandmother's key. He decided to give it a bit longer this time, and while he was waiting he lay down in bed. He began counting to ten slowly. He got roughly as far as five before he fell asleep.

He was woken at dawn by Little Bull bawling at him.

The Indian was standing outside the felt tepee on the edge of the table, his hands cupped to his mouth as if shouting across a measureless canyon. As soon as Omri's eyes opened, the Indian shouted:

"Day come! Why you still sleep? Time eat – hunt – fight – make painting!"

Omri leapt up. He cried, "Wait" – and almost wrenched the cupboard open.

There on the shelf stood a small tepee made of real leather. Even the stitches on it were real. The poles were twigs, tied together with a strip of hide. The designs were real Indian symbols, put on with bright dyes.

The car was still a toy car made of metal, no more real than it had ever been.

"It works," breathed Omri. And then he caught his breath. "Little Bull!" he shouted. "It works, it works! I can make any plastic toy I like come alive, come real! It's real magic, don't you understand? Magic!"

The Indian stood calmly with folded arms, evidently disapproving of this display of excitement.

"So? Magic. The spirits work much magic. No need wake dead with howls like coyote."

Omri hastily pulled himself together. Never mind the dead, it was his parents he must take care not to wake. He picked up the new tepee and set it down beside the one he had made the night before.

"Here's the good one I promised you," he said.

Little Bull examined it carefully. "No good," he said at last.

"What? Why not?"

"Good tepee, but no good Iroquois brave. See?" He pointed to the painted symbols. "Not Iroquois signs. Algonquin.

Enemy. Little Bull sleep there, Iroquois spirits angry."

"Oh," said Omri, disappointed.

"Little Bull like Omri tepee. Need paint. Make strong pictures – Iroquois signs. Please spirits of ancestors."

Omri's disappointment melted into intense pride. He had made a tepee which satisfied his Indian! "It's not finished," he said. "I'll take it to school and finish it in my handicrafts lesson. I'll take out the pins and sew it up properly. Then when I come home I'll give you poster-paints and you can paint your symbols."

"I paint. But must have longhouse. Tepee no good for Iroquois."

"Just for now?"

Little Bull scowled. "Yes," he said. "But very short. Now eat."

"Er... Yes. What do you like to eat in the mornings?"

"Meat," said the Indian immediately.

"Wouldn't you like some bread and cheese?"

"Meat."

"Or corn? Or some egg?"

The Indian folded his arms uncompromisingly across his chest.

"Meat," said Omri with a sigh. "Yes. Well, I'll have to see what I can do. In the meantime, I think I'd better put you down on the ground."

"Not on ground now?"

"No. You're high above the ground. Go to the edge and look – but don't fall!"

The Indian took no chances. Lying on his stomach he crawled, commando-fashion, to the edge of the chest-of-drawers and peered over.

"Big mountain," he commented at last.

"Well…" But it seemed too difficult to explain. "May I lift you down?"

Little Bull stood up and looked at Omri measuringly. "Not hold tight?" he asked.

"No. I won't hold you at all. You can ride in my hand."

He laid his hand palm up next to Little Bull, who, after only a moment's hesitation, stepped on to it and, for greater stability, sat down cross-legged. Omri gently transported him to the floor. The Indian rose lithely to his feet and jumped off on to the grey carpet.

At once he began looking about with suspicion. He dropped to his knees, felt the carpet and smelt it.

"Not ground," he said. "Blanket."

"Little Bull, look up."

He obeyed, narrowing his eyes and peering.

"Do you see the sky? Or the sun?"

The Indian shook his head, puzzled.

"That's because we're not outdoors. We're in a room, in

a house. A house big enough for people my size. You're not even in America. You're in England."

The Indian's face lit up. "English good! Iroquois fight with English against French!"

"Really?" asked Omri, wishing he had read more. "Did you fight?"

"Fight? Little Bull fight like mountain lion! Take many scalps."

Scalps? Omri swallowed. "How many?"

Little Bull proudly held up all ten fingers. Then he closed his fists, opening them again with another lot of ten, and another.

"I don't believe you killed so many people!" said Omri, shocked.

"Little Bull not lie. Great hunter. Great fighter. How show him son of Chief without many scalps?"

"Any white ones?" Omri ventured to ask.

"Some. French. Not take English scalps. Englishmen friends to Iroquois. Help Indian fight Algonquin enemy."

Omri stared at him. He suddenly wanted to get away. "I'll go and get you some — meat," he said in a choking voice.

He went out of his room, closing the bedroom door behind him.

For a moment he did not move, but leant back against

the door. He was sweating slightly. This was a bit more than he had bargained for!

Not only was his Indian no mere toy come to life; he was a real person, somehow magicked out of the past of over two hundred years ago. He was also a savage. It occurred to Omri for the first time that his idea of Red Indians, taken entirely from Western films, had been somehow false. After all, those had all been actors playing Indians, and afterwards wiping their war-paint off and going home for their dinners, not in tepees but in houses like his. Civilized men, pretending to be primitive, pretending to be cruel...

Little Bull was no actor. Omri swallowed hard. Thirty scalps... phew! Of course things were different in those days. Those tribes were always making war on each other, and come to that the English and French (whatever they thought they were doing, fighting in America) were probably no better, killing each other like mad as often as they could...

Come to *that*, weren't soldiers of today doing the same thing? Weren't there wars and battles and terrorism going on all over the place? You couldn't switch on television without seeing news about people killing and being killed... Was thirty scalps, even including some French ones, taken hundreds of years ago, so very bad after all?

Still, when he tried to imagine Little Bull, full size, bent over some French soldier, holding his hair in one hand and running the point of his scalping-knife… Yuk!

Omri pushed away from the door and walked rather unsteadily downstairs. No wonder he had felt, from the first, slightly afraid of his Indian. He asked himself, swallowing repeatedly and feeling that just the same he might be sick, whether he wouldn't do better to put Little Bull back in the cupboard, lock the door and turn him back into plastic, knife and all.

Down in the kitchen he ransacked his mother's store-cupboard for a tin of meat. He found some corned beef at last and opened it with the tin-opener on the wall. He dug a chunk out with a teaspoon, put it absently into his own mouth and stood there chewing it.

The Indian hadn't seemed very surprised about being in a giant house in England. He had shown that he was very superstitious, believing in magic and good and evil spirits. Perhaps he thought of Omri as – well, some kind of genie, or whatever Indians believed in instead. The wonder was that he wasn't more frightened of him then, for genies, or giants, or Great Spirits, or whatever, were always supposed to be very powerful and often wicked. Omri supposed that if one happened to be the son of an Indian Chief, one simply didn't get scared as easily as ordinary people. Especially, perhaps, if one had taken thirty scalps…

Maybe Omri ought to tell someone about Little Bull.

The trouble was that although grown-ups usually knew what to do, *what* they did was very seldom what children wanted to be done. What if he took the Indian to – say, some scientists, or – whoever knew about strange things like that, to question him and examine him and probably keep him in a laboratory or something of that sort? They would certainly want to take the cupboard away too, and then Omri wouldn't be able to have any more fun with it at all.

Just when his mind was seething with ideas, such as putting in plastic bows and arrows, and horses, and maybe even other little people – well, no, probably that was too risky, who knew what sort you might land up with? They might start fighting each other! But still, he knew for certain he didn't want to give up his secret, not yet, no matter how many Frenchmen had been scalped.

Having made his decision, for the moment anyway, Omri turned to go upstairs, discovering only halfway up that the tin of corned beef was practically empty. Still, there was a fair-sized bit left in the bottom. It ought to do.

Little Bull was nowhere to be seen, but when Omri called him softly he ran out from under the bed, and stood waving both arms up at Omri.

"Bring meat?"

"Yes." Omri put it on the miniature plate he'd cut the

night before and placed it before the Indian, who seized it in both hands and began to gnaw on it.

"Very good! Soft! Your wife cook this?"

Omri laughed. "I haven't got a wife."

The Indian stopped and looked at him. "Omri not got wife? Who grow corn, grind, cook, make clothes, keep arrows sharp?"

"My mother," said Omri, grinning at the idea of her sharpening arrows. "Have you got a wife then?"

The Indian looked away. After a moment he said, "No."

"Why not?"

"Dead," said Little Bull shortly.

"Oh."

The Indian finished eating in silence and then stood up, wiping his greasy hands on his hair. "Now. Do magic. Make things for Little Bull."

"What do you want?"

"Gun," he answered promptly. "White man's gun. Like English soldier."

Omri's brain raced. If a tiny knife could stab, a tiny gun could shoot. Maybe it couldn't do much harm, but then again, maybe it could.

"No, no gun. But I can make you a bow and arrows. I'll have to buy plastic ones, though. What else? A horse?"

"Horse!" Little Bull seemed surprised.

"Don't you ride? I thought all Indians rode."

Little Bull shook his head.

"English ride. Indians walk."

"But wouldn't you like to ride, like the English soldiers?"

Little Bull stood quite still, frowning, wrestling with this novel idea. At last he said, "Maybe. Yes. Maybe. Show horse. Then I see."

"Okay."

Again Omri rummaged in the biscuit tin. There were a number of horses here. Big heavy ones for carrying armoured knights. Smaller ones for pulling gun-carriages in the Napoleonic wars. Several cavalry horses – those might be the best. Omri ranged five or six of various sizes and colours before Little Bull, whose black eyes began to shine.

"I have," he said promptly.

"You mean all of them?"

Little Bull nodded hungrily.

"No, that's too much. I can't have herds of horses galloping all over my room. You can choose one."

"One?" said Little Bull sadly.

"One."

Little Bull then made a very thorough examination of every horse, feeling their legs, running his hands over their rumps, looking straight into their plastic faces. At last he selected a smallish, brown horse with two white feet which had originally (as far as Omri could remember) carried an Arab, brandishing a curved sword at a platoon of French Foreign Legionnaires.

"Like English horse," grunted Little Bull.

"And he's got a saddle and bridle, which will become real too," gloated Omri.

"Little Bull not want. Ride with rope, bare-back. Not like white soldier," he added contemptuously, having another spit. "When?"

"I still don't know how long it takes. We can start now."

Omri lifted the cupboard onto the floor, shut the horse in and turned the key. Almost at once they could hear the clatter of tiny hooves on metal. They looked at each other with joyful faces.

"Open! Open door!" commanded Little Bull.

Omri lost no time in doing so. There, prancing and pawing the white paint, was a lovely, shiny-coated little brown Arab pony. As the door swung open he shied nervously, turning his face and pricking his ears so far forward they almost met over his forelock. His tiny nostrils flared, and his black tail plumed over his haunches as he gave a high, shrill neigh.

Little Bull cried out in delight.

In a moment he had vaulted over the bottom edge of the cupboard and, as the pony reared in fright, jumped into the air under its flying hooves and grasped the leather reins. The pony fought to free its head, but Little Bull hung on with both hands. Even as the pony plunged and bucked, the Indian had moved from the front to the side. Grasping the high pommel of the saddle he swung himself into it. He ignored the swinging stirrups, holding on by gripping with his knees.

The pony flung himself back on his haunches, then threw himself forward in a mighty buck, head low, heels flying. To Omri's dismay, Little Bull, instead of clinging on somehow, came loose and flew through the air in a curve, landing on the carpet just beyond the edge of the cupboard.

Omri thought his neck must be broken, but he had landed in a sort of somersault, and was instantly on his feet again. The face he turned to Omri was shining with happiness.

"Crazy horse!" he cried with fierce delight.

The crazy horse was meanwhile standing quite still, reins hanging loose, looking watchfully at the Indian through wild, wide-apart eyes.

This time Little Bull made no sudden moves. He stood quite still for a long time, just looking back at the pony. Then, so slowly you could scarcely notice, he edged towards him, making strange hissing sounds between his clenched teeth which almost seemed to hypnotize the pony. Step by step he moved, softly, cautiously, until he and the pony stood almost nose to nose. Then, quite calmly, Little Bull reached up and laid his hand on the pony's neck.

That was all. He did not hold the reins. The pony could have jumped away, but he didn't. He raised his nose a little, so that he and the Indian seemed to be breathing into each other's nostrils. Then, in a quiet voice, Little Bull said, "Now horse mine. Crazy horse mine."

Still moving slowly, though not as slowly as before, he took the reins and moved alongside the pony. After a certain amount of fiddling he found out how to unbuckle the straps which held the Arabian saddle, and lifted it off, laying it on the floor. The pony snorted and tossed his head, but did not move. Hissing gently now, the Indian first leant his weight against the pony's side, then lifted himself up by his arms until he was astride. Letting the reins hang loose on the pony's neck, he squeezed with his legs. The pony moved forward, as tame and obedient as you please, and the pair rode once round the inside of the cupboard as if it had been a circus arena.

Suddenly Little Bull caught up the reins and pulled them to one side, turning the pony's head. At the same time Little Bull kicked him sharply. The pony wheeled, and bounded forward towards the edge of the cupboard.

This metal rim, about two centimetres high, was up to the pony's chest — like a five-barred gate to a full-sized horse. There was no room to ride straight at it, from the back of the cupboard to the front, so Little Bull rode diagonally – a very difficult angle, yet the pony cleared it in a flying leap.

Omri realized at once that the carpet was too soft for him – his feet simply sank into it like soft sand.

"Need ground. Not blanket," said Little Bull sternly. "Blanket no good for ride."

Omri looked at his clock. It was still only a little after six in the morning – at least another hour before anyone else would be up.

"I could take you outside," he said hesitantly.

"Good!" said Little Bull. "But not touch pony. You touch, much fear."

Omri quickly found a small cardboard box which had held a Matchbox lorry. It even had a sort of window through which he could see what was happening inside. He laid that on the carpet with the end flaps open.

Little Bull rode the pony into the box, and Omri carefully shut the end up and even more carefully lifted it. Then, in his bare feet, he carried the box slowly down the stairs and let himself out through the back door.

It was a lovely fresh summer morning. Omri stood on the back steps with the box in his hands, looking round for a suitable spot. The lawn wasn't much good – the grass would be over the Indian's head in most places. The terrace at the foot of the steps was no use at all, with its hard uneven bricks and the cracks between them. But the path was beaten earth and small stones — real riding-ground if they were careful. Omri walked to the path and laid the Matchbox carton down.

For a moment he hesitated. Could the Indian run away? How fast could such a small pony run? As fast as, say, a mouse? If so, and they wanted to escape, Omri wouldn't be able to catch them. A cat, on the other hand, would. Omri knelt on the path in his pyjamas and put his face to the Cellophane 'window'. The Indian stood inside holding the pony's head.

"Little Bull," he said clearly, "we're outdoors now. I'm going to let you out to ride. But remember — you're not on your prairie now. There are mountain lions here, but they're big enough to swallow you whole and the pony too. Don't run away, you wouldn't survive. Do you understand?"

Little Bull looked at him steadily and nodded. Omri opened the flap and Indian and pony stepped out into the morning sunlight.

Chapter Four

THE GREAT OUTDOORS

BOTH HORSE AND man seemed to sniff the air, tasting its freshness and testing it for danger at the same time. The pony was still making circles with his nose when Little Bull sprang onto his back.

The pony, startled, reared slightly, but this time Little Bull clung on to his long mane. The pony's front feet had no sooner touched the path than he was galloping. Omri leapt to his feet and gave chase.

The pony's speed was remarkable, but Omri found that by running along the lawn beside the path he could keep up quite easily. The ground was dry and as Indian and pony raced along, a most satisfying cloud of dust rose behind them so that Omri could easily imagine that they were galloping across some wild, unbroken territory...

More and more, he found, he was able to see things from the Indian's point of view. The little stones on the path became huge boulders which had to be dodged, weeds became trees, the lawn's edge an escarpment twice the height of a man... As for living things, an ant, scuttling across the pony's path, made him shy wildly. The shadow of a passing bird falling on him brought him to a dead stop, crouching and cowering as a full-sized pony might if some huge bird of prey swooped at him. Once again, Omri marvelled at the courage of Little Bull, faced with all these terrors.

But it was not the courage of recklessness. Little Bull clearly recognized his peril and, when he had had his gallop, turned the pony's head and came trotting back to Omri, who crouched down to hear what he said.

"Danger," said the Indian. "Much. I need bow, arrows, club. Maybe gun?" he asked pleadingly. Omri shook his head. "Then Indian weapons."

"Yes," said Omri. "You need those. I'll find them today. In the meantime we'd better go back in the house."

"Not go shut-in place! Stay here. You stay, drive off wild animals."

"I can't. I've got to go to school."

"What school?"

"A place where you learn."

"Ah! Learn. Good," said Little Bull approvingly. "Learn law of tribe, honour for ancestors, ways of the spirits?"

"Well… something like that."

Little Bull was clearly reluctant to return to the house, but he had the sense to realize he couldn't cope outside by himself. He galloped back along the path, with Omri running alongside, and dismounting, re-entered the carton.

Omri was just carrying it up the back steps when the back door suddenly opened and there was his father.

"Omri! What on earth are you doing out here in your pyjamas? And nothing on your feet, you naughty boy! What are you up to?"

Omri clutched the box to him so hard in his fright that he felt the sides bend and quickly released his hold. He felt himself break into a sweat.

"Nothing – I – couldn't sleep. I wanted to go out."

"What's wrong with putting on your slippers, at least?"

"Sorry. I forgot."

"Well, hurry up and get dressed now."

Omri rushed upstairs and, panting, laid the box on the floor. He opened the flap. The pony rushed out alone, and stood under the table, whinnying and trembling – he had had a rough ride. Full of foreboding, Omri bent down and peered into the box. Little Bull was sitting in a corner of it, hugging his leg, which Omri saw, to his horror, was bleeding right through his buckskin leggings.

"Box jump. Pony get fear. Kick Little Bull," said the Indian, who, though calm, was clearly in pain.

"Oh, I'm sorry!" cried Omri. "Can you come out? I'll see what I can do."

Little Bull stood up and walked out of the box. He did not let himself limp.

"Take off your leggings – let me see the cut," said Omri.

The Indian obeyed him and stood in his breech-cloth. On his tiny leg was a wound from the pony's hoof, streaming blood onto the carpet. Omri didn't know what to do, but Little Bull did.

"Water," he ordered. "Cloths."

Omri, through his panic, forced himself to think clearly. He had water in a toothmug by his bed, but that would not be clean enough to wash a wound. His mother had some Listerine in her medicine cupboard; when any of the boys had a cut she would add a few drops to some warm water and that was a disinfectant.

Omri dashed to the bathroom, and with trembling hands did what he had seen his mother do. He took a small piece of cotton-wool. What could be used as a bandage he had no idea at all. But he hurried back with the water, and poured some into the Action Man's mess-tin. The Indian tore off a minute wisp of cotton-wool and dipped it into the liquid and applied it to his leg.

The Indian's eyes opened wide though he did not wince. "This not water! This fire!"

"It's better than water."

"Now tie," said the Indian next. "Hold in blood."

Omri looked round desperately. A bandage small enough for a wound like that! Suddenly his eyes lighted on the biscuit tin. There, lying on top, was a First World War soldier with the red armband of a medical orderly. In his hand was a doctor's bag with a red cross on it. What might that contain if Omri could make it real?

Not stopping to think too far ahead, he snatched the figure up and thrust it into the cupboard, shutting the door and turning the key.

A moment later a thin English voice from inside called: "Here! Where am I? Come back you blokes – don't leave a chap alone in the dark!"

Chapter Five

TOMMY

OMRI FELT HIMSELF grow weak. What an idiot he'd been! Not to have realized that the man and not just the medical bag would be changed! Or had he? After all, what did he need more just then than a bandage of the right size for the Indian? *Someone* of the right size to put it on! And, unless he was sadly mistaken, that was just what was waiting inside the magic cupboard.

He unlocked the door.

Yes, there he was – pink cheeked, tousle-headed under his army cap, his uniform creased and mud-spattered and blood-stained, looking angry, frightened and bewildered.

He rubbed his eyes with his free hand.

"Praise be for a bit of daylight, anyway," he said. "What the—"

Then he opened his eyes and saw Omri.

Omri actually saw him go white, and his knees gave way under him. He uttered a few sounds, half curses and half just noises. He dropped the bag and hid his face for a moment. Omri said hastily:

"Please don't be afraid. It's all right. I—" Then he had an absolute inspiration! "I'm a dream you're having. I won't hurt you, I just want you to do something for me, and then you'll wake up."

Slowly the little man lowered his hands and looked up again.

"A dream, is it? Well... I should've guessed. Yes, of course. It would be. The whole rotten war's nightmare enough, though, without giants and – and—" He stared round Omri's room. "Still and all, perhaps it's a change for the better. At least it's quiet here."

"Can you bring your bag and climb out? I need your help."

The soldier now managed a rather sickly smile and tipped his cap in a sort of salute. "Right you are! With you in a tick," he said, and picking up the bag, clambered over the edge of the cupboard.

"Stand on my hand," Omri commanded.

The soldier did not hesitate a moment, but swung himself up by hooking his free arm round Omri's little finger. "Bit of a lark, this," he remarked. "I won't half enjoy telling the fellows about this dream of mine in the trenches tomorrow!"

Omri carried him to the spot where Little Bull sat on the carpet holding his leg which was still bleeding. The soldier stepped down and stood, knee-deep in carpet-pile, staring.

"Well, I'll be jiggered!" he breathed. "A bloomin' redskin! This is a rum dream and no mistake! And wounded, too. Well, I suppose that's my job, is it? – to patch him up?"

"Yes, please," said Omri.

Without more ado, the soldier put the bag on the floor and snapped open its all-but-invisible catches. Omri leant over to see. Now he really did need a magnifying glass, and so badly did he want to see the details of that miniature doctor's bag that he risked sneaking into Gillon's room (Gillon always slept late, and anyway it wasn't seven o'clock yet) and pinching his from his secret drawer.

By the time he got back to his own room, the soldier was kneeling at Little Bull's feet, applying a neat tourniquet to the top of his leg. Omri peered through the magnifying glass into the open bag. It was amazing – everything was there, bottles, pill-boxes, ointments, some steel instruments including a tiny hypodermic needle, and as many rolls of bandages as you could want.

Omri then ventured to look at the wound. Yes, it was quite deep – the pony must have given him a terrific kick.

That reminded him – where was the pony? He looked round in a fright. But he soon saw it, trying forlornly to eat the carpet. "I must get it some grass," thought Omri, meanwhile offering it a small piece of stale bread which it ate gratefully, and then some water in a tin lid. It was odd how the pony was not frightened of him. Perhaps it couldn't see him very well.

"There now, he'll do," said the soldier, getting up.

Omri looked at the Indian's leg through his magnifying glass. The wound was bandaged beautifully. Even Little Bull was examining it with obvious approval.

"Thank you very much," said Omri. "Would you like to wake up now?"

"Might as well, I suppose. Not that there's much to look forward to except mud and rats and German shells coming over… Still. Got to win the war, haven't we? Can't desert, even into a dream, not for long that is – duty calls and all that, eh?"

Omri gently picked him up and put him into the cupboard.

"Goodbye," he said. "Perhaps, some time, you could dream me again."

"A pleasure," said the soldier cheerfully. "Tommy Atkins, at your service. Any night, except when there's an attack on – none of us gets any sleep to speak of then." And he gave Omri a smart salute.

Regretfully Omri shut and locked the door. He was tempted to keep the soldier, but it was too complicated just now. Anyway he could always bring him back to life again if he liked… A moment or two later he opened the door again to check. There was the orderly, bag in hand, standing just as Omri had last seen him, at the salute. Only now he was plastic again.

Little Bull was calmly pulling on his blood-stained leggings.

"Good magic," he remarked. "Leg better."

"Little Bull, what will you do all day while I'm at school?"

"You bring bark of tree. Little Bull make longhouse."

"What's that?"

"Iroquois house. Need earth, stick posts in."

"*Earth? Posts?*"

"Earth. Posts. Bark. Not forget food. Weapons. Tools. Pots. Water. Fire—"

There were no quarrels at breakfast that morning. Omri gulped down his egg and ran. In the greenhouse he found a seed-tray already full of soil, well pressed down. He carried that secretly upstairs and laid it on the floor behind the dressing-up crate, which he was pretty sure his mother wouldn't shift even if it was her cleaning day. Then he took his penknife and went out again.

Fortunately one of the trees in the garden had the sort

of bark which came off easily – a silvery, flaky kind. He cut off a biggish strip, and then another to make sure (how long *was* a longhouse?). He pulled some grass for the pony. He cut a bundle of thin, strong, straight twigs and stripped off their leaves. Then he went back to his room and laid all these offerings beside Little Bull, who was seated cross-legged outside his tepee, arms folded, eyes closed, apparently saying his prayers.

"Omri!" came his mother's call from downstairs. "Time to go!"

Omri took out of his pocket the corner of toast he'd saved from breakfast and cleaned out the last of the corned beef from the tin. There was some corn left as well, though it was getting rather dry by now. He filled up the Action Man's beaker with water from the bathroom, pouring a little into the pony's drinking-lid. The pony was munching the fresh grass with every sign of enjoyment. Omri noticed its bridle had been replaced with a halter, cleverly made of a length of thread.

"Omri!"

"Just coming!"

"The others have gone! Hurry up, you'll be late!"

One last thing! Little Bull couldn't make a longhouse without some sort of tool beside his knife. He'd need an axe. Frantically Omri rummaged in the biscuit tin. Ah!

A knight, wielding a fearsome-looking battle axe. It wasn't right, but it was better than nothing and would have to do. In a second the knight was locked in the cupboard.

"*Omri!*"

"One second!"

"What are you *doing*?"

Crash! The axe was being used on the inside of the cupboard door!

Omri wrenched it open, snatched the axe from the startled hands of the knight, who had just time for one horrified look before he was reduced to plastic again by the slamming of the door. Never mind! He had looked most unpleasant, just as knights must have looked when they were murdering the poor Saracens in Palestine. Omri had very little time for knights.

The axe was a beauty, though. Shining steel, with a sharp edge on both sides of the head, and a long heavy steel handle. Omri laid it at Little Bull's side.

"Little Bull—"

But he was still in a trance – communicating with his ancestors, Omri supposed. Well, he would find everything when he came to. There was quite a trail of spilt earth leading behind the crate. Omri flashed down the stairs, grabbed his anorak and his lunch-money and was gone.

Chapter Six

THE CHIEF IS DEAD,
LONG LIVE THE CHIEF

HE GOT TO school early by running all the way. The first thing he did was to head for the upper school library shelves. He felt that a Ladybird book on Indian tribes would not meet the situation; he wanted a much more grown-up book. And to his joy, he soon found one, under the section labelled 'Peoples of the World' – a book called *On the Trail of the Iroquois*.

He couldn't take it out because there was nobody there to write him down for it; but he sat down then and there on a bench and began to read it.

Omri was not what you'd call a great reader. He couldn't get into books, somehow, unless he knew them already. And how, as his teacher never tired of asking, was he ever going to get to know any more books until he read them for the first time?

And this *On the Trail of the Iroquois* was not exactly a comic. Tiny print, hardly any pictures, and no fewer than three hundred pages. 'Getting into' it was obviously out of the question, so Omri just dipped.

He managed to find out one or two fairly interesting things straight away. Iroquois Indians were sometimes called 'The Five Nations'. One of the five were the Mohawks, a tribe Omri had heard of. They had indeed lived in longhouses, not wigwams, and their main foods had been maize and squash (whatever they were) and beans. These vegetables had, for some strange reason, been called 'The Three Sisters'.

There were many mentions of the Algonquins as the Iroquois' enemies, and Omri confirmed that the Iroquois had fought beside the English while the Algonquins fought for the French some time in the 1700s, and that both sides had scalped like mad.

At this point he began to get really interested. The book, in its terribly grown-up way, was trying to tell him something about *why* the Indians had done such a lot of scalping. Omri had always thought it was just an Indian custom, but the book seemed to say that it wasn't at all, at least not till the White Man came. The White Man seemed to have made the Iroquois and the Algonquin keen on scalping each other, not to mention scalping White Men, French or English as the case might be, by offering them money and whisky, and guns… Omri was deep in the book, frowning heavily, several minutes after the bell had rung. Someone had to tap him on the shoulder and tell him to hurry in to Assembly.

The morning lasted forever. Three times his teacher had cause to tell Omri to wake up. At last Patrick leant over and whispered, "You're even dreamier than usual today. What's up?"

"I'm thinking about your Indian."

"Listen," hissed Patrick. "I think you're having me on about that Indian. It was nothing so marvellous. You can buy them for a few pence in Yapp's." (Yapp's was their local newsagent and toyshop.)

"I know, and all the equipment for them! I'm going shopping at lunchbreak; are you coming?"

"We're not allowed out of school at lunch unless we eat at home, you know that!"

"I'm going anyway. I've got to."

"Go after school."

"No, I've got to go home after school."

"What? Aren't you staying to skateboard?"

"*Omri and Patrick!* Will you kindly stop chattering?"

They stopped.

At long last lunchtime came.

"I'm going. Are you coming?"

"No. There'll only be trouble."

"I can't help that."

"You're a twit."

Twit or not, Omri sneaked out, ran across the playground, through a hole in the fence (the front gate was locked to keep the infants from going in the road) and in five minutes, by running all the way, had reached Yapp's.

The selection of plastic figures there was good. There was one whole box of mixed cowboys and Indians. Omri searched till he found a Chief wearing a cloak and a full feather headdress, with a bow in his hand and a quiverful of arrows slung across his back. Omri bought it with part of his lunch money and rushed back to school before he could be missed.

He showed the Chief to Patrick.

"Why get another Indian?"

"Only for the bow and arrows."

Patrick was now looking at him as if he'd gone completely screwy.

In the afternoon, mercifully, they had two periods of handicrafts.

Omri had completely forgotten to bring the tent he'd

made, but there were plenty of scraps of felt, sticks, needles and thread lying about the handicrafts room and he'd soon made another one, much better than the first. Sewing had always bored him rigid, but now he sat for half an hour stitching away without even looking up. He was trying to achieve the patched look of a real tepee made of odd-shaped pieces of hide, and he also found a way of bracing the sticks so that they didn't fold up every time they were nudged.

"Very good, Omri!" remarked his teacher several times. "What patience all of a sudden!" Omri, who usually liked praise as much as anyone, hardly heard her, he was concentrating so hard.

After a long time he became aware that Patrick was standing over him, breathing through his nose rather noisily to attract his attention.

"Is that for my Indian?"

"*My* Indian. Yes."

"Why are you doing it in bits like that?"

"To be like a real one."

"Real ones have designs on."

"So will this. He's going to paint proper Iroquois ones."

"Who is?"

"Little Bull. That's his name."

"Why not call him Running Nose?" asked Patrick with a grin.

Omri looked up at him blankly. "Because his name's Little Bull," he said. Patrick stopped grinning. He frowned.

"I wish you'd stop this stupid business," he said peevishly. "Going on as if it weren't a joke."

Omri went on looking at him for a moment and then went back to his bracing. Each pair of sticks had to have another, short stick glued between them with Airfix glue. It was quite tricky. Patrick stood a minute and then said, "Can I come home with you today?"

"No. I'm sorry."

"Why not?"

"Mum's having guests," Omri mumbled. He didn't tell lies very well, and Patrick knew at once it was a lie and was hurt.

"Oh, all right then, be like that," he said, and stalked off furiously.

The afternoon ended at last. Omri accomplished the walk home, which with normal dawdling took half an hour, in a little over ten minutes. He arrived sorely out of breath and greeted his surprised mother ("Have you developed a jet-engine, or have you been expelled?") with a lot of gasping and a request to eat tea in his room.

"What have you been up to, up there? There's an awful mess on the floor – looks like bits of grass and bark. And where did you get that beautiful little Indian tepee? I think it's made of real leather."

Omri looked at her, speechless. "I—" he began at last. Telling lies to Patrick was one thing. Lying to his mother was quite something else and he never did it unless the emergency was dire. But mercifully the phone rang just then, so he was spared – for the moment. He dashed upstairs.

There was indeed a fair old mess, though no worse than he often left himself when he'd been working on something. Little Bull and the pony were nowhere to be seen, but Omri guessed where to look – behind the dressing-up crate.

A wonderful sight met his eyes. A longhouse – not quite finished, but no less interesting and beautiful for that – stood on the seed-box, whose smooth surface was now much trampled over. There were hoof- as well as moccasin-prints. Omri saw that a ramp, made of part of the bark, had been laid against the wooden side of the box, up which the pony had been led – to Omri's delight (odd as it may seem) a tiny pile of horse-manure lay on the ramp as proof of the pony's passing. And there he was, tied by a thread to an upright twig hammered (presumably) into the ground, munching a small pile of grass which the Indian had carried up for him.

Little Bull himself was still working, so intently that he did not even notice he was not alone. Omri watched him in utter fascination. The longhouse was about half finished. The twigs, which had been pliant ones taken from the weeping-willow on the lawn, had been stripped of their bark, leaving them shining white. Each one had then been bent into an arch, the ends thrust into the earth, and cross-pieces lashed to the sides with thread. More and more twigs (which were stout poles to the Indian) had been added, with never a nail or a screw needed, to strengthen the structure, and now Little Bull had begun to fix flakes of bark like tiny tiles, on to the cross-pieces.

He was seated on the roof itself, his feet locked round the main roof-pole which ran the length of the house hanging these bark-tiles, each of which he would first carefully shape with his knife. The knight's battle-axe lay on the ground beside an unused pile of twigs. It had clearly been used to chop and strip them and had been made to serve Little Bull's purpose very well.

At last Omri saw him straighten up, stretch his arm towards the ceiling, and open his mouth in a tremendous noisy yawn.

"Tired?" he asked him.

Little Bull got such a fright he almost fell off the longhouse roof, and the pony neighed and tugged at his rope. But then Little Bull looked up and saw Omri hanging over the crate far above him, and grinned.

"Little Bull tired. Work many hour. Look! Make longhouse. Work for many braves. I make alone. Also not good tools. Axe Omri give heavy. Why no tomahawk?"

Omri was getting used to his Indian's ungrateful ways and was not offended. He showed him the tepee he'd made. "I suppose you won't want this, now you've got your longhouse," he said rather sadly.

"Want! Want!" He seemed to have decided tepees had their uses after all. He circled it. "Good! Give paints. Make pictures."

Omri unearthed his poster paints. When he came back with them, he found Little Bull sitting cross-legged on the earth, facing the figure of the Chief which Omri had put next to the tepee. Little Bull was clearly puzzled.

"Totem?" he asked.

"No! It's plastic."

"Plass-tick?"

"Yes. I bought it in a shop."

Little Bull stared at the figure with its big feather headdress.

"You make magic, get bow and arrows from plass-tick?"

"Yes."

"Also make feathers real?" he asked, with a gleam in his eye.

"You like that headdress?"

"Little Bull like. But that for Chief. Little Bull not Chief till father die. Little Bull wear feathers of Chief now, spirits angry."

"But you could just try it on?"

Little Bull looked doubtful but he nodded.

"Make real. Then see."

Omri shut the Indian Chief into the cupboard. Before he turned the key, he leant down to where Little Bull was examining the (to him) enormous pots of paint.

"Little Bull, are you lonely?"

"Huh?"

"Would you like a — friend?"

"Got friend," said the Indian, jerking his head towards the pony.

"I meant, another Indian."

Little Bull looked up swiftly, his hands still. There was a long silence.

"Wife?" he asked at last.

"No, it's a man," said Omri. "The — Chief."

"Not want," said Little Bull immediately, and went back to his work with a bent head.

Omri was disappointed. He had thought it might be fun to have two Indians. But somehow he couldn't do anything Little Bull didn't want. He would have to treat this Chief as he had treated the knight — grab the weapons and turn him back into plastic again at once.

Only this time it wasn't quite so easy.

When he opened the cupboard, the Chief was sitting on the shelf, looking about him in bewilderment, blinking as the light struck his eyes. Omri saw at once that he was a very old man, covered in wrinkles. He took the bow out of his hands quite easily. But the quiverful of arrows was hung round him on a leather thong, and as for actually lifting the feathered headdress off his grey old head, Omri found he just couldn't bring himself to do it. It seemed so rude.

The old man gazed up at him, blankly at first, and then with dawning terror. But he didn't get up and he didn't speak, though Omri saw his lips moving and noticed he had hardly any teeth.

Omri somehow felt he should offer the old Chief some friendly word to reassure him. So he held up one hand, as white men sometimes did in films when they were treating Indian Chiefs with politeness, and said, "How."

The old Indian lifted a trembling hand, and then suddenly he slumped on to his side.

"Little Bull! Little Bull! Quick, get on to my hand!"

Omri reached down and Little Bull climbed on to his hand from the longhouse roof.

"What?"

"The old Indian – I think he's fainted!"

He carried Little Bull to the cupboard and Little Bull stepped off on to the shelf. He stooped beside the crumpled figure. Taking the single feather out of the back of his own headband he held it in front of the old man's mouth. Then he shook his head.

"Dead," he said. "No breath. Heart stop. Old man. Gone to ancestors, very happy." Without more ado, he began to strip the body, taking the headdress, the arrows, and the big, richly-decorated cloak for good measure.

Omri was shocked.

"Little Bull, stop. Surely you shouldn't—"

"Chief dead; I only other Indian here. No one else to be Chief. Little Bull Chief now," he said, whirling the cloak about his own bare shoulders and clapping the splendid circle of feathers on to his head with a flourish. He picked up the quiver.

"Omri give bow!" he commanded. And it was a command. Omri obeyed it without thinking. "Now! You make magic. Deer for Little Bull hunt. Fire for cook. Good meat!" He folded his arms, scowling up at Omri.

Omri was quite taken aback by all this. While giving Little Bull every respect as a person, he was not about to be turned into his slave. He began to wonder if giving him those weapons, let alone letting him make himself into a Chief, was such a good idea.

"Now look here, Little Bull—" he began, in a teacherish tone.

"OMRI!"

It was his father's voice, fairly roaring at him from the foot of the stairs. Omri jumped, bumping the cupboard. Little Bull fell over backwards, considerably spoiling his dignity.

"Yes?"

"COME DOWN HERE THIS INSTANT!"

Omri had no time for courtesies. He snatched Little Bull up, set him down near his half-finished longhouse, shut and locked the cupboard and ran downstairs.

His father was waiting for him.

"Omri, have you been in the greenhouse lately?"

"Er—"

"And did you, while you were there, remove a seed-tray planted out with marrow seeds, *may I ask?*"

"Well, I—"

"Yes or no."

"Well, yes, but—"

"And is it possible that in addition you have been hacking at the trunk of the birch and torn off strips of bark?"

"But Dad, it was only—"

"Don't you know trees can *die* if you strip too much of their bark off? It's like their skin! As for the seed-tray, that is *mine*. You've no business taking things from the greenhouse and you know it. Now I want it back, and you'd better not have disturbed the seeds or heaven help you!"

Omri swallowed hard. He and his father stared at each other.

"I can't give it back," he said at last. "But I'll buy you another tray and some more seeds. I've got enough money. *Please.*"

Omri's father had a quick temper, especially about anything concerning the garden, but he was not unreasonable, and above all he was not the sort to pry into his children's secrets. He realized at once that his seed-tray, as a seed-tray, was lost to him forever and that it was no use hectoring Omri about it.

"All right," he said. "You can go to the hardware shop and buy them, but I want them today."

Omri's face fell.

"Today? But it's nearly five o'clock now."

"Precisely. Be off."

Chapter Seven

UNINVITED BROTHERS

OMRI WAS NOT allowed to ride his bicycle in the road, but then he wasn't supposed to ride it on the pavement either, not fast at any rate, so he compromised. He rode it slowly on the pavement as far as the corner, then bumped down off the curb and went like the wind.

The hardware shop was still open. He bought the seed-tray and the seeds and was just paying for them when he noticed something. On the seed packet, under the word 'Marrow' was written another word in brackets: 'Squash'.

So one of the 'Three Sisters' was marrow! On impulse he asked the shopkeeper, "Do you know what maize is?"

"Maize, son? That's sweetcorn, isn't it?"

"Have you some seeds of that?"

Outside, standing by Omri's bike, was Patrick.

"Hi."

"Hi. I saw you going in. What did you get?"

Omri showed him.

"More presents for the Indian?" Patrick asked sarcastically.

"Well, sort of. If—"

"If what?"

"If I can keep him long enough. Till they grow."

Patrick stared at him and Omri stared back.

"I've been to Yapp's," said Patrick. "I bought you something."

"Yeah? What?" asked Omri, hopefully.

Slowy Patrick took his hand out of his pocket, held it in front of him and opened the fingers. In his palm lay a cowboy on a horse, with a pistol in one hand pointing upward, or what would have been upward if it hadn't been lying on its side.

Omri looked at it silently. Then he shook his head.

"I'm sorry. I don't want it."

"Why not? Now you can play a proper game with the Indian."

"They'd fight."

"Isn't that the whole idea?"

"They might hurt each other."

There was a pause, and then Patrick leant forward and

asked, very slowly and loudly, "*How can they hurt each other? They are made of plastic!*"

"Listen," said Omri, and then stopped, and then started again. "The Indian isn't plastic. He's real."

Patrick heaved a deep, deep sigh and put the cowboy back in his pocket. He'd been friends with Omri for years, ever since they'd started school. They knew each other very well. Just as Patrick knew when Omri was lying, he also knew when he wasn't. The only trouble was that this was a non-lie he couldn't believe.

"I want to see him," he said.

Omri debated with himself. He somehow felt that if he didn't share his secret with Patrick, their friendship would be over. He didn't want that. And besides, the thrill of showing his Indian to someone else was something he could not do without for much longer.

"Okay. Come on."

Going home they broke the law even more, riding on the road *and* with Patrick on the crossbar. They went round the back way by the alley in case anyone happened to be looking out of a window.

Omri said, "He wants a fire. I suppose we can't make one indoors."

"You could, on a tin plate, like for indoor fireworks," said Patrick.

Omri looked at him.

"Let's collect some twigs."

Patrick picked up a twig about a foot long. Omri laughed.

"That's no good! They've got to be tiny twigs. Like this." And he picked some slivers off the privet hedge.

"Does he want the fire to cook on?" asked Patrick slowly.

"Yes."

"Then that's no use. A fire made of those would burn out in a couple of seconds."

Omri hadn't thought of that.

"What you need," said Patrick, "is a little ball of tar. That burns for ages. And you could put the twigs on top to look like a real campfire."

"That's a brilliant idea!"

"I know where they've been tarring a road, too," said Patrick.

"Come on, let's go."

"No."

"Why not?"

"I don't believe in him yet. I want to see."

"All right. But first I have to give this stuff to my dad."

There was a further delay when his father at first insisted on Omri filling the seed-tray with compost and planting the seeds in it then and there. But when Omri gave him the corn seed as a present he said, "Well! Thanks. Oh, all right, I can see you're bursting to get away. You can do the planting tomorrow before school."

Omri and Patrick rushed upstairs. At the top Omri stopped, cold. His bedroom door, which he always shut automatically, was wide open. And just inside, crouching side by side with their backs to him, were his brothers.

They were so absolutely still that Omri knew they were watching something. He couldn't bear it. They had come into his room without his permission, and they had seen his Indian. Now they would tell everybody! His secret, his precious secret, his alone to keep or share, was a secret no more. Something broke inside him and he heard himself scream: "Get out of my room! Get out of my room!"

Both boys spun round.

"Shut up, you'll frighten him," said Adiel at once. "Gillon came in to look for his rat and he found it, and then he saw this absolutely fabulous little house you've made and he called me in to look at it."

Omri looked at the floor. The seed-tray, with the longhouse now nearly finished, had been moved into the centre of the room. It was *that* they had been looking at. A quick glance all round showed no sign of Indian or pony, but Gillon's tame white rat was on his shoulder.

"I can't get over it," Adiel went on. "How on earth did you do it, without using any Airfix glue or anything? It's all done with tiny little threads, and pegs, and − look, Gillon! It's all made of real twigs and bark. It's absolutely *terrific*," he said with such awe-struck admiration in his voice that Omri felt ashamed.

"I didn't—" he began. But Patrick, who had been gaping at the longhouse in amazement, gave him a heavy nudge which nearly knocked him over.

"Yes," said Omri. "Well. Would you mind pushing off now? And take the rat. You're not to let him in here! This *is* my room, you know."

"And this *is* my magnifying glass, you know," echoed Gillon, but he was obviously too overcome with admiration to be angry with Omri for pinching it. He was using it now to examine the fine details of the building. "I knew you were good at making things," he said. "But this is amazing. You must have fingers like a fairy to tie those *witchy* little knots. What's that?" he asked suddenly.

They'd all heard it − a high, faint whinny coming from under the bed.

Omri was galvanized into action. At all costs he must prevent their finding out now! He flung himself on his knees and pretended to grope under the bed. "It's nothing, only that little clockwork dolphin I got in my

Christmas stocking," he burbled. "I must have wound it up and it suddenly started clicking, you know how they do, it's quite creepy sometimes when they suddenly start – clicking—"

By this time he'd leapt up again and was almost pushing the two older boys out of the room.

"Why are you in such a hurry to get rid of us?" asked Gillon suspiciously.

"Just *go*, you know you have to get out of my room when I ask you—" He could hear the pony whinnying again and it didn't sound a bit like a dolphin.

"That sounds just like a pony," said Adiel.

"Oh, *beard* it's a pony, a tiny witchy pony under my bed!" said Omri mockingly.

At last they went, not without glancing back suspiciously several times, and Omri slammed the door, bolted it, and leant against it with closed eyes.

"*Is* it a pony?" whispered Patrick, agog.

Omri nodded. Then he opened his eyes, lay down again, and peered under the bed.

"Give me that torch from the chest-of-drawers."

Patrick gave it to him and lay beside him. They peered together as the torch-beam probed the darkness.

"Crumbs!" breathed Patrick reverently. "It's true!"

The pony was standing, seemingly alone, whinnying.

When the torchlight hit him he stopped and turned his head. Omri could see a pair of leggings behind him.

"It's all right, Little Bull, it's me!" said Omri.

Slowly a crest of feathers, then the top of a black head, then a pair of eyes appeared over the pony's back.

"Who they others?" he asked.

"My brothers. It's okay, they didn't see you."

"Little Bull hear coming. Take pony, run, hide."

"Good. Come on out and meet my friend Patrick."

Little Bull jumped astride the pony and rode proudly out, wearing his new cloak and headdress. He gazed up imperiously at Patrick, who gazed back in wonder.

"Say something to him," whispered Omri. "Say 'How'. That's what he's used to."

Patrick tried several times to say 'How' but his voice just came out as a squeak. Little Bull solemnly raised an arm in salute.

"Omri's friend, Little Bull's friend," he said magnanimously.

Patrick swallowed. His eyes seemed in danger of popping right out of his head.

Little Bull waited politely, but when Patrick didn't speak he rode over to the seed-tray. The boys had brought it out from behind the crate; they'd been careful, but the ramp had got moved. Omri hurried to put it back, and

Little Bull rode the pony up it, dismounted and tied it by its halter to the post he had driven into the compost. Then he went calmly on with his work on his longhouse, hanging the last few tiles.

Patrick licked his lips, swallowed twice more, and croaked out, "He's real. He's a real live Indian."

"I told you."

"How did it happen?"

"Don't ask me. Something to do with this cupboard, or maybe it's the key – it's very old. You lock plastic people inside, and they come alive."

Patrick goggled at him. "You mean – it's not only him? You can do it with any toy?"

"Only plastic ones."

An incredulous grin spread over Patrick's face.

"Then what are we waiting for? Let's bring loads of things to life! Whole armies—"

And he sprang towards the biscuit tins. Omri grabbed him.

"No, wait! It's not so simple."

Patrick, his hands already full of soldiers, was making for the cupboard. "Why not?"

"Because they'd all – don't you see – they'd be *real*."

"Real? What do you mean?"

"Little Bull isn't a toy. He's a real man. He really lived. Maybe he's still – I don't know – he's in the middle of his life — somewhere in America in seventeen-something-or-other. He's from the past," Omri struggled to explain as Patrick looked blank.

"I don't get it."

"Listen. Little Bull has told me about his life. He's fought in wars, and scalped people, and grown stuff to eat like marrows and stuff, and had a wife. She died. He doesn't know how he got here but he thinks it's magic and he accepts magic, he believes in it, he thinks I'm some kind of spirit or something. What I mean," Omri persisted, as Patrick's eyes strayed longingly to the cupboard, "is that if you put all those men in there, when they came to life they'd be real men with real lives of their own, from their own times and countries, talking their own languages. You couldn't just — set them up and make them do what you wanted them to. They'd do what *they* wanted to, or they might get terrified and run away or — well, one I tried it with, an old Indian, actually died of — of fright. When he saw me. Look, if you don't believe me!" And Omri opened the cupboard.

There lay the body of the old Chief, now made of plastic, but still unmistakably dead, and not dead the way some plastic soldiers are made to look dead but the way real people look — crumpled up, empty.

Patrick picked it up, turning it in his hand. He'd put the soldiers down by now.

"This isn't the one you bought at lunchtime?"

"Yes."

"Crumbs."

"You see?"

"Where's his headdress?"

"Little Bull took it. He says he's a Chief now. It's made him even more bossy and – *difficult* than before," said Omri, using a word his mother often used when he was insisting on having his own way.

Patrick put the dead Indian down hurriedly and wiped his hand on the seat of his jeans.

"Maybe this isn't such fun as I thought."

Omri considered for a moment.

"No," he agreed soberly. "It's not *fun.*"

They stared at Little Bull. He had finished the shell of the longhouse now. Taking off his headdress he tucked it under his arm, stooped, and entered through the low doorway at one end. After a moment he came out and looked up at Omri.

"Little Bull hungry," he said. "You get deer? Bear? Moose?"

"No."

He scowled. "I say get. Why you not get?"

"The shops are shut. Besides," added Omri, thinking he sounded rather feeble, especially in front of Patrick, "I'm not sure I like the idea of having bears shambling about my room, *or* of having them killed. I'll give you meat and a fire and you can cook it and that'll have to do."

Little Bull looked baffled for a moment. Then he swiftly put on the headdress, and drew himself to his full height of seven centimetres (nearly eight with the feathers). He folded his arms and glared at Omri.

"Little Bull Chief now. Chief hunts. Kills own meat. Not take meat others kill. If not hunt, lose skill with bow. For today, you give meat. Tomorrow, go shop, get bear, plass-tick. Make real. I hunt. Not here," he added, looking up scornfully at the distant ceiling. "Out. Under sky. Now fire."

Patrick, who had been crouching, stood up. He, too, seemed to be under Little Bull's spell.

"I'll go and get the tar," he said.

"No wait a minute," said Omri. "I've got another idea."

He ran downstairs. Fortunately the living-room was empty. In the coal-scuttle beside the open fireplace was a packet of firelighters. He broke a fairly large bit off one and wrapped it in a scrap of newspaper. Then he went to the kitchen. His mother was standing at the sink peeling apples.

Omri hesitated, then went to the fridge.

"Don't eat now, Omri, it's nearly suppertime."

"Just a tiny bit," he said.

There was a lovely chunk of raw meat on a plate. Omri

sniffed his fingers, wiped them hard on his sweater to get the stink of the firelighter off them, then took a big carving-knife from the drawer and, with an anxious glance at his mother's back, began sawing a corner off the meat.

Luckily it was steak and cut easily. Even so he nearly had the whole plate off the fridge shelf and onto the floor before he'd cut his corner off.

His mother swung round just as he closed the fridge door.

"A tiny bit of what?" she asked. She often reacted late to things he said.

"Nothing," he said, hiding the raw bit of meat in his hand. "Mum, could I borrow a tin plate?"

"I haven't got such a thing."

"Yes you have, the one you bought Adiel to go camping."

"That's in Adiel's room somewhere, I haven't got it. A tiny bit of *what*?"

But Omri was already on his way upstairs. Adiel was in his room (he would be) doing his homework.

"What do *you* want?" he asked the second Omri crept in.

"That plate – you know – your camping one."

"Oh, that!" said Adiel, going back to his French.

"Well, can I have it?"

"Yeah, I suppose so. It's over there somewhere."

Omri found it eventually in an old knapsack, covered with disgusting bits of baked beans, dry and hard as cement.

He hurried across to his own room. Whenever he'd been away from it for even a few minutes, he felt his heart beating in panic as he opened the door for fear of what he might find (or not find). The burden of constant worry was beginning to wear him out.

But all was as he had left it this time. Patrick was crouching near the seed-tray. Little Bull was directing him to take the tops off several of the jars of poster paint while he himself fashioned something almost too small to see.

"It's a paintbrush," whispered Patrick. "He cut a bit of his own hair and he's tying it to a scrap of wood he found about the size of a big splinter."

"Pour a bit of paint into the lids so he can reach to dip," said Omri.

Meanwhile he was scraping the dry beans off the plate with his nails. He took the fragment of firelighter and the privet-twigs out of his pocket and arranged them in the centre of the plate. He washed the bit of meat in his bedside water glass. He'd had a wonderful idea for a spit to cook it on. From a flat box in which his first Meccano set had once been neatly laid out, but which was not in chaos, he took a rod, ready bent into a handle shape, and pushed this through the meat. Then, from small bits of Meccano, he quickly made a sort of stand for it to rest on, with legs each side of the fire so that the meat hung over the middle of it.

"Let's light it now!" said Patrick, who was getting very excited again.

"Little Bull – come and see your fire," said Omri.

Little Bull looked up from his paints and then ran down the ramp, across the carpet and vaulted onto the edge of the plate. Omri struck a match and lit the firelighter, which flared up at once with a bluish flame, engulfing the twigs and the meat at once. The twigs gave off a gratifying crackle while they lasted, but the firelighter gave off a very ungratifying stench which made Little Bull wrinkle up his nose.

"Stink!" he cried. "Spoil meat!"

"No it won't!" Omri said. "Turn the handle of the spit, Little Bull."

Evidently he wasn't much used to spits, but he soon got the hang of it. The chunk of steak turned and turned in the flame, and soon lost its raw red look and began to go grey and then brown. The good juicy smell of roasting beef began to compete with the reek of the firelighter.

"Mmm!" said Little Bull appreciatively, turning the handle till the sweat ran off his face. "Meat!" He had thrown off his Chief's cloak and his chest shone red. Patrick couldn't take his eyes off him.

"Please Omri," he whispered, "couldn't I have one? Couldn't I choose just one – a soldier, or anything I liked – and make him come to life in your cupboard?"

Chapter Eight

COWBOY!

OMRI GAPED AT him. He hadn't thought of this, but of course now that he did it was obvious – no boy who knew the secret could possibly rest until he had a little live person of his own.

"Patrick – it's not like you think – just something to play with—"

"Of course not, you've explained all about it, now just let me put—"

"But you have to think about it first. No, no, stop, you can't yet! And anyway I don't agree to you using one of mine!" Omri didn't know why he was so reluctant. It wasn't that he was mean. He just knew, somehow, that something awful would happen if he let Patrick have his own way. But it wasn't easy to stop him. Omri had grabbed him, but he wrenched free.

"I've got to—" he panted. "I've got to—"

He stretched out his hand towards the pile of soldiers again. They struggled. Patrick seemed to have gone a bit crazy. Suddenly Omri felt the rim of the tin plate under his shifting feet.

He shoved Patrick out of the way and they both stared downward. The plate had tipped, the fire slipped on to the carpet. Little Bull, with a yell, had leapt clear, and was now waving his arms and shouting horrible things at them. His roast meat had disappeared under Omri's foot, which instinctively stamped down on the fire to put it out. Omri felt the Meccano crunching under his school shoe, and a squishy feeling…

"Now look! We've spoilt the meat!" he shouted at Patrick. "If all you can do is fight, I wish I'd never brought you!"

Patrick looked mulish. "It was your fault. You should have let me put something in the cupboard."

Omri lifted his shoe. Underneath was a nasty mess of burnt stuff, squashed meat and bent Meccano. Little Bull let out a wail.

"You no great spirit! Only stupid boy! Fight, spoil good meal! You feel shame!"

"Maybe we can rescue it—"

He crouched down and disentangled the meat from the mess, burning his fingers. He tried to brush it clean but it was no use – it was all mixed up with the smelly stuff of the firelighter, and stuck with bits of carpet hairs.

"I'm terribly sorry, Little Bull," he mumbled.

"No good sorry! Little Bull hungry, work all day, cook meat – now what eat? I chop you down like tree!" And to Omri's horror he saw Little Bull run to where the battleaxe was lying, pick it up and advance towards his leg, swinging it in great circles as he came.

Patrick fairly danced with excitement. "Isn't he fantastically brave, though! Much more than David with Goliath!"

Omri felt the whole thing was going too far. He removed his leg from harm's way. "Little Bull! Calm down," he said. "I've said I'm sorry."

Little Bull looked at him, blazing-eyed. Then he rushed over to the chair Omri used at his table and began chopping wedges out of the leg of it.

"Stop! Stop! Or I'll put you back in the cupboard!"

Little Bull stopped abruptly and dropped the axe. He stood with his back to them, his shoulders heaving.

"I'll get you something to eat – right now – something delicious. Go and paint. It'll make you feel better. I won't be long." To Patrick he said, "Hang on. I can smell supper cooking, I'll go and get a bit of whatever we're having," and he rushed downstairs without stopping to think.

His mother was dishing up a nice hot stew.

"Can I have a tiny bit of that, Mum? Just a little bit, in a spoon. It's for a game we're playing."

His mother obligingly gave him a big spoonful. "Don't let it drip," she said. "Does Patrick want to stay for supper?"

"I don't know – I'll ask," said Omri.

"Were you two fighting up there? I heard thumps."

"No-o – not really. It was just that he wanted to do something that I—"

Omri stopped dead, as if frozen to the ground. He might have been frozen, his face went so cold. Patrick was up there – with the cupboard – and two biscuit-tinsful of little plastic figures – alone!

He ran. He usually won the egg-and-spoon race at the school sports, which was just as well – it's hard enough to carry an egg in a spoon running along a flat field; it's a great deal harder to carry a tablespoonful of boiling hot stew steady while you rush up a flight of stairs. If most of it was still there when he got to the top it was more by good luck than skill because he was hardly noticing the spoon at all – all he could think of was what might be – no, *must* be happening in his room, and how much more of it would happen if he didn't hurry.

He burst in through the door and saw exactly what he'd dreaded – Patrick, bent over the cupboard, just turning the key to open it.

"What—" Omri gasped out between panting breaths, but he had no need to go on. Patrick, without turning round, opened the cupboard and reached in. Then he did turn. He was gazing into his cupped hands with eyes like huge marbles. He slowly extended his hands towards Omri, and whispered, "Look!"

Omri, stepping forward, had just time to feel intensely glad that at least Patrick had not put a whole handful of figures in but had only changed one. But which? He leant over, then drew back with a gasp.

It was the cowboy. And his horse.

The horse was in an absolute panic. It was scrambling about wildly in the cup of Patrick's hand, snorting and pawing, up one minute and down on its side the next, stirrups and reins flying. It was a beautiful horse, snow-white with a long mane and tail, and the sight of it acting so frightened gave Omri heart-pains.

As for the cowboy, he was too busy dodging the horse's flying feet and jumping out of the way when he fell to notice much about his surroundings. He probably thought he was caught in an earthquake. Omri and Patrick watched, spellbound, as the little man in his plaid shirt, buckskin trousers, high-heeled leather boots and big hat, scrambled frantically up the side of Patrick's right hand and, dodging through the space between his index finger and thumb, swung himself clear of the horse – only to look down and find he was dangling over empty space.

His hat came off and fell, slowly like a leaf, down, down, down to the floor so infinitely far below. The cowboy gave a yell, and scrabbled with his feet against the back of Patrick's hand, hanging on for dear life to the ridge beside his thumb-nail.

"Hold your hands still!" Omri commanded Patrick, who in his excitement was jerking them nervously about. There was a moment of stillness. The horse stood up, trembling all over, prancing about with terror. Beside his hooves was some tiny black thing. Omri peered closer. It was the pistol.

The cowboy had now recovered a little. He scrambled back through the finger-gap and said something to the horse which sounded like "Whoaback, steady, fella." Then he slid down and grabbed the reins, holding them just below the horse's nose. He patted its face. That seemed to calm it. Then, looking round swiftly but not apparently noticing the enormous faces hanging over him, he reached cautiously down and picked the pistol up from between the horse's hooves.

"Whoa there! Stand—"

Omri watched like a person hypnotized. He wanted to cry out to Patrick that it was a real gun, but somehow he couldn't. He could only think that the sound of his voice would throw the horse once more into a panic and the horse or man would get hurt. Instead he watched while the cowboy pointed the gun in various directions warily. Then he lowered it.

Still holding the reins he moved until he could press his hand against Patrick's skin. Then he let his eyes move upward towards the curved fingers just level with the top of his head.

"What the dawggone heck—" he said. "It sure looks like a great big – Aw, what'm Ah talkin' about? It cain't be. Hell, it just ain't possible!" But the more he looked, the more certain he must have become that he was, indeed, in a pair of cupped hands. And finally, after scratching his gingery head for a moment, he ventured to look right up past the fingers, and then of course he saw Patrick's face looking at him.

There was a petrified moment when he couldn't move. Then he raised his pistol in a flash.

"Patrick! Shut your eyes!"

Bang!

It was only a little bang, but it was a real bang, and a puff of real, gun-smelling smoke appeared. Patrick shouted with pain and surprise and would have dropped the pair if Omri hadn't thrust his hand underneath to catch them. Patrick's own hand had clapped itself to his cheek.

"Ow! Ow! He's shot me!" Patrick screamed.

Omri was not much bothered about Patrick at that moment. He was furious with him, and very anxious about the little man and his horse. Quickly he put them down on the bed, saying, like the cowboy himself, "Steady! Whoa! I won't hurt you! It's okay!"

"Ow!" Patrick kept yelling. "It hurts! Ow!"

"Serve you right, I warned you," said Omri. Then he felt sorry and said, "Let's have a look."

Gingerly Patrick took his hand down. A drop of blood had been smeared on his cheek, and by peering very close Omri could see something very like a bee's sting embedded in his skin.

"Hang on! I see it – I'll squeeze it out—"

"OW!"

A quick squeeze between his thumbnails and the almost invisible speck of black metal, which had only just penetrated the skin, popped out.

"He – shot me!" Patrick got out again in a shocked voice.

"I *told* you. My Indian stuck a knife in me," said Omri, not to be outdone. "I think we ought to put him back – your cowboy I mean, of course, not my Indian."

"Put him back where?"

Omri explained how the cupboard could change him back to plastic again, but Patrick wasn't having any of that.

"Oh no! I want him! He's terrific. Look at him now—"

Patrick feasted his eyes admiringly on the little cowboy. Ignoring the 'giants', whom he clearly thought he must have imagined, he was doggedly dragging his horse across Omri's quilt as if he were wading through the dunes of some infinite pale-blue desert.

Omri reached for him determinedly, but Patrick stepped into his path.

"Don't you touch him! I bought him, I changed him – he's mine!"

"You bought him for me!"

"You said you didn't want him."

"Well, but the cupboard's mine, and I told you not to use it."

"And so what if I did? Anyway, it's done, he's alive now and I'm keeping him. I'll bash you right in if you try to take him. Wouldn't you bash me if I took your Indian?"

Omri was silent. That reminded him! Where was Little Bull? He looked round. He soon spotted him at the other side of the room, busy with his paints. Some beautiful minute designs, showing turtles and herons and beavers, mainly in red and yellow, had appeared on the side of the tepee Omri had made. As Omri crouched beside him to admire them, Little Bull, without looking at him, said "You bring food? I very soon die if not eat."

Omri looked around. What had he done with the spoonful of stew? But he soon saw that he'd put it down on the table without thinking. There it sat, tilting slightly and spilling a few drops of gravy, but still steaming. He hurried to get Little Bull's – or rather the Action Man's – mess-tin (the paper plate had got all soggy) and carefully filled it with the hot savoury stuff.

"Here you are."

Little Bull stopped work, laid down his paintbrush, and sniffed eagerly.

"Ah! Good!" He sat down cross-legged among the paint lids to eat, dipping some of yesterday's stale bread in as a spoon. "Your wife cook? Ah. No. Little Bull forgot. Omri not got wife." He ate ravenously for a few moments and then said, "Not want?"

"I'm having mine downstairs in a minute," Omri said.

"Mean, Omri not want wife," said Little Bull, who was now in a much better mood.

"I'm not old enough."

Little Bull looked at him for a moment. "No. I see. Boy." He grinned. "Big boy, but boy." He went on eating. "Little Bull want," he said finally, not looking up.

"Another wife?"

"Chief needs wife. Beautiful. Good cook. Act as told." He put his face into the mess-tin and licked it clean. Then he looked up.

"With Iroquois, mother find wife for son. But Little Bull's mother not here. Omri be mother and find."

Omri couldn't quite see himself as Little Bull's mother, but he said, "I might try. I think there were some Indian women in Yapp's. But what if I get one and make her real and then you don't fancy her?"

"Fancy?"

"Like her."

"I like. Young. Beautiful. Act as told. I like. So you get."

"Tomorrow."

Little Bull grinned at him happily, his face smeared with gravy.

Patrick had come up behind him.

"Let's put them together and see what they do!"

Omri jumped up quickly.

"No!"

"Why *not*?"

"You idiot, because yours has got a gun and mine's got a bow and arrow and one of them's sure to kill the other!"

Patrick considered this. "Well, we could take their weapons away from them. Come on, I'm going to!" And he reached towards the bed.

Just at that moment there was the sound of steps on the stairs. They froze. Then Omri swiftly moved the dressing-up crate enough to hide Little Bull, and Patrick sat down on the end of the bed, masking the poor cowboy who was still toiling along over the lumps in the quilt.

Just in time! Omri's mother opened the door next second and said, "Patrick, that was your mum on the phone. She wants you to come home right away. And Omri – it's supper." And she went.

Omri opened his mouth to protest, but Patrick at once said, "Oh, okay." With one quick movement he had scooped up cowboy and horse in his left hand and thrust them into his blazer pocket. Omri winced – he could easily imagine the horse's legs being injured by such rough treatment, not to mention the matter of fright. But Patrick was already halfway out of the door.

Omri jumped up and grabbed his arm.

"Patrick!" he whispered. "You must be careful! Treat them carefully! They're *people* – I mean they're alive – what will you do with them? How will you hide them from your family?"

"I won't, I'll show them to my brother anyway, he'll go out of his mind."

Omri began to think he might go out of his. He shook Patrick's arm. "*Will you think?* How are you going to explain? What will happen? If you say you got him from me I'll do worse than bash you – you'll ruin everything – they'll take the cupboard away—"

That got through to Patrick at last. He put his hand slowly back into his pocket.

"Listen then. You can look after them. But remember – they're mine. If you put them back in the cupboard, I'll tell everyone. I'm warning you. I will. Bring them to school tomorrow."

"To school!" cried Omri aghast. "I'm not bringing Little Bull to school!"

"You can do what you like about Little Bull, he's yours. The cowboy's mine, and I want him at school tomorrow, otherwise I'll tell."

Omri let go of his arm and for a moment they looked at each other as if they'd been strangers. But they weren't strangers; they were friends. That counts for a lot in this life. Omri gave in.

"All right," he said, "I'll bring them. Now give them to me. *Gently*." And Patrick brought man and horse out of his pocket and tipped them very carefully into Omri's waiting hand.

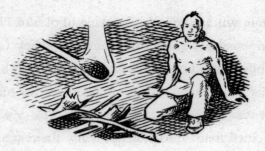

Chapter Nine

SHOOTING MATCH

OMRI PUT THE cowboy and horse in his shirt drawer while he had the quickest supper on record. Then he raced upstairs again, stopping only to pinch a few grains of Gillon's rat feed for the two horses.

Shut up in his room, he took stock. A room this size was like a sort of indoor national park to the cowboy and the Indian. It should be easy enough to keep them apart for one night. Omri thought first of putting the new pair straight back in the cupboard, and then bringing them back to life next morning in time for school, but he had promised Patrick not to. So he decided to empty out the dressing-up crate and put the cowboy and his horse in there for the night.

The crate was a metre square, made of planks. There was certainly no visible way out of it for the cowboy. Omri put him carefully down into it. Looking at him, he felt curious – about his name, where he came from and so on; but he decided it was better not to talk to him. The cowboy had clearly decided that Omri was not really there at all. When his big hands reached down, carrying some cold stew, grain for the pony, some fragments of apple for them both and, later, some cottonwool and scraps of material for bedding, the cowboy deliberately covered his eyes by pulling down his big hat brim. It was only when Omri reached in one final time to give him a drink of water in a minute green glass bottle that he had found in the bathroom cupboard, that the cowboy spoke a word.

"Take that filthy stuff outa here!" he suddenly shouted, in his strong Texas accent. "Ah ain't aimin' to drink no more o' that as lawng as Ah live!" And he heaved the bottle (which was almost as big as himself) up by its base and tipped its contents out onto the boards at the bottom of the crate.

"It's only water," Omri ventured to say.

"You shet yer mouth!" shouted the little man. "Ah won't take no lip from no gol-darned hallucy-nation, no sir! Mebbe Ah do drink too much, mebbe Ah cain't hold m'likker like some o' them real tough guys do. But if'n Ah'm gittin' the dee-lirium tremens, and startin' in to see things, why couldn't Ah see pink elly-fants and dancin' rats and all them purty things other fellas see when they gits far gone? It ain't fair fer me to see giants and blue deserts and git put in boxes the size of the Grand Canyon with no one but m'little hoss for comp'ny!" He sat down on the pile of hay, took the horse's nose in his arms, put his face against it and began to sob.

Omri was shattered. A cowboy – crying! He didn't know what to do. When his mother cried, as she did sometimes when things got too much, she only asked to be left alone till she felt better. Maybe all grown-ups were like that. Omri turned away and got slowly into his pyjamas, and then went to see how Little Bull was getting along on the far side of the crate.

He'd finished the painting. The tepee looked really good. Little Bull was now in the longhouse, arranging his blanket for the night. The pony was tethered to his post on a long rope. Omri took out the rat food and gave it to him. Then he called Little Bull out.

"Are you okay? Anything you need?"

He should have known better than to ask.

"Plenty! Want fire in longhouse, keep warm, keep wild animals away. Want tomahawk—"

"So you can chop bits out of my leg?"

"Little Bull angry when say that. Sorry now. Use tomahawk cut down trees, chop firewood, kill bird—"

"What bird?"

Little Bull replied with a very good imitation of a cock crowing. Then he did a mime of catching it, putting its neck on to a block, and, with a whirl of his arm, chopping off its head with gleeful relish.

"I don't know about that!"

"You get. Tomorrow. Birds from plass-tick. Good tools. But fire — now. Chief Little Bull say!"

Omri sighed. He went to the waste paper basket and picked out the remains of the other fire that he'd thrown away in there. There was quite a lot of the firelighter left. He gathered up some of the bits of willow-bark and twigs from where Little Bull had been working.

"You're not having it inside, though — far too dangerous!"

He arranged the fire on the packed earth of the seed-tray, about fifteen centimetres from the entrance to the longhouse, first moving the tepee to safety. Then he struck a match and soon there was a cosy blaze.

Little Bull crouched beside it, his red skin glowing and his eyes bright with pleasure.

"Little Bull, can you dance?"

"Yes. War dance, wedding dance, many kind."

"Would you do one now so I can see?"

He hesitated, then he shook his head once.

"Why not, though?"

"No make war, no make wedding. No reason dance."

"Maybe if I got you a wife—"

The Indian looked up eagerly. "You get? Give word?"

"I only said I'd try."

"Then Little Bull dance. Then do best dance — love dance."

Omri turned off his light and drew back from the scene. It looked amazingly real, with the fire making shadows, the little horse munching his grain and the Indian sitting on his heels warming himself, wearing his colourful headdress and the Chief's cloak. Omri wished he himself were small enough to join Little Bull by the fire.

"Om-ri! Are you in bed? I'm coming up in five minutes to kiss you goodnight!"

Omri felt panicky. But it was all right. The fire was going out. Already Little Bull was standing up, yawning and stretching. He peered up through the darkness.

"Hey, Omri! Paintings good?"

"Great!"

"You sleep now?"

"Yes."

"Peace of great spirits be on you."

"Thanks, same to you."

Omri peered quickly into the crate. The poor cowboy had crawled away into his makeshift bed and was snoring loudly. He hadn't eaten a thing. Omri sighed. He hoped Patrick was making plans and arrangements. After all, if Omri could keep his Indian secret, Patrick might be able to do the same. All might yet be well. But Omri certainly wasn't going to try the experiment again. It was all just too much worry.

He climbed into bed, feeling unusually tired. His mother came in and kissed him, and the door was shut. He felt himself drifting off almost right away.

When suddenly, a piercing whinny sounded. And was answered by another.

The horses had smelt each other!

They were not so far apart — and the cowboy's wasn't tied up. Omri could hear his little hooves clattering on the bare boards of the crate, and then the whinnies began again, high, shrill — almost questioning. Omri thought of putting on his light, but he was awfully tired — besides, what could he do? They couldn't possibly reach each other through the planks of the crate wall. Let them whinny their heads off, they'd soon get fed up.

Omri rolled over and fell asleep.

He was woken just after dawn by shots.

He was out of bed in about one-fifth of a second. One glance into the crate showed him all too clearly that the cowboy and his horse had escaped. The second glance showed how – a knot in the wood had been pushed out (or perhaps kicked out by the horse) leaving an oval-shaped hole like an arched doorway, just big enough to let horse and rider through.

Omri looked round wildly. At first he could see nothing. He dropped to his knees beside the seed-tray and peered into the longhouse. Little Bull was not there – nor was his pony.

Suddenly some tiny thing whizzed past Omri's ear and struck the crate beside him with a ping! Twisting his head, Omri saw it – a feathered arrow the size of a pin, still quivering from its flight.

Was Little Bull shooting at *him*?

"Little Bull! Where are you?"

No answer. But suddenly, a movement, like that of a mouse, caught the corner of his eye. It was the cowboy. Dragging his horse behind him, he was running, half bent over, from behind one chair-leg to another. He had his revolver in his hand, his hat on his head. Another arrow flew, missing the crate this time and burying itself in the carpet – just ahead of the running cowboy, who stopped dead, jumped backwards till his horse hid him, and then fired another two shots from behind the horse's shoulder.

Omri, following his aim, spotted Little Bull at once. He and his pony were behind a small heap of cloth which was like a snow-covered hill to them but was actually Omri's vest, dropped carelessly on the floor the night before. Little Bull, safe in the shelter of this cotton mountain, was just preparing to shoot another arrow at the cowboy, one which could hardly fail to hit its mark. The poor fellow was now scrambling desperately on to his pony to try and ride away and was in full sight of the Indian as he drew back his bowstring.

"Little Bull! Stop!"

Omri's voice rang out frenziedly. Little Bull did not stop; but his surprise spoilt his aim, and the arrow sped over the cowboy, doing no worse than sweep away his big hat and pin it to the skirting-board behind the chair.

This infuriated the little man, who, forgetting his fear, stood up in his stirrups and shouted, "Tarnation take ya, ya red varmint! Wait'll Ah ketch ya. Ah'll have yer stinkin' red hide for a sleepin' bag!"

With that he rode straight towards the vest-hill at full gallop, shouting out strange cowboy-like war cries and waving his gun, which, by Omri's count, still had two bullets in it.

Little Bull had not expected this, but he was only outfaced for a moment. Then he coolly drew another arrow from his quiver and fitted it to his bow.

"Little Bull, if you shoot I'll pick you up and *squeeze* you!" Omri cried.

Little Bull kept his arrow pointing towards the oncoming horseman.

"What you do if he shoot?" he asked.

"He won't shoot! Look at him."

Sure enough, the carpet was too soft for much galloping, and even as Omri spoke the cowboy's horse stumbled and fell, pitching its rider over its head.

Little Bull lowered his bow and laughed. Then, to Omri's horror, he laid down the bow among the folds of the vest, reached for his knife, and began to advance on the prostrate cowboy.

"Little Bull, you are not to touch him, do you hear?"

Little Bull stopped. "He try to shoot Little Bull. White enemy. Try take Indian's land. Why not kill? Better dead. I act quick, he not feel, you see!" And he began to move forward again.

When he was nearly up to the cowboy Omri swooped on him. He didn't squeeze him of course, but he did lift him high and fast enough to give him a fright.

"Listen to me now. That cowboy isn't after your land. He's got nothing to do with you. He's Patrick's cowboy, like you're my Indian. I'm taking him to school with me today, so you won't be bothered by him any more. Now you take your pony and get back to your longhouse and leave him to me."

Little Bull, sitting cross-legged in the palm of his hand, gave him a sly look.

"You take him to school? Place you learn about ancestors?"

"That's what I said."

He folded his arms offendedly. "Why you not take Little Bull?"

Omri was startled into silence.

"If white fool with coward's face good enough, Indian Chief good enough."

"You wouldn't enjoy it—"

"If him enjoy, I enjoy."

"I'm not taking you. It's too risky."

"Risky! Fire-water?"

"Not *whisky* – risky. Dangerous."

He shouldn't have said that. Little Bull's eyes lit up.

"Like danger! Here too quiet. No hunting, no enemy, only *him*," he said scornfully, peering over the edge of Omri's hand at the cowboy, who, despite the softness of his landing-place, was only just scrambling to his feet. "Look! Him no use for fight. Little Bull soon kill, take scalp, finish. Very good scalp," he added generously. "Fine colour, look good on belt."

Omri looked across at the cowboy. He was leaning his ginger head against his saddle. It looked as if he might be crying again. Omri felt very sorry for him.

"You're not going to hurt him," he said to the Indian, "because I won't let you. If he's such a coward, it wouldn't do your honour any good anyway."

Little Bull's face fell, then grew mulish. "No tell from scalp on belt if belong to coward or brave man," he said slyly. "Let me kill and I do dance round campfire," he coaxed.

"No—" Omri began. Then he changed his tactics. "All right, you kill him. But then I won't bring you a wife."

The Indian looked at him a long time. Then he slowly put his knife away.

"No touch. Give word. Now you give word. Take Little Bull to school. Take to plass-tick. Let Little Bull choose own woman."

Omri considered. He could keep Little Bull in his pocket all day. No need to take any chances. If he were tempted to show the other children, well, he must resist temptation, that was all.

And after school he could take him to Yapp's. The boxes with the plastic figures in them were in a corner behind a high stand. Provided there weren't too many other kids in the shop, he might be able to give Little Bull a quick look at the Indian women before he bought one, which would be a very good thing. Otherwise he might pick an old or ugly one without realizing it. It was so hard to see from their tiny plastic faces what they would be like when they came to life.

"Okay then, I'll take you. But you must do as I tell you and not make any noise."

He put him down on the seed-tray and gently shooed the pony up the ramp. Little Bull tied it to its post and Omri gave it some more rat food. Then he crawled on hands and knees over to where the cowboy was now sitting dolefully on the carpet, his horse's rein looped round his arm, looking too miserable to move.

"What's the matter?" Omri asked him.

The little man didn't look up. "Lost muh hat," he mumbled.

"Oh, is that all?" Omri reached over to the skirting-board and pulled the pin-like arrow out of the wide brim of the hat. "Here it is," he said kindly, laying it in the cowboy's lap.

The cowboy looked at it, looked up at Omri, then stood up and put the hat on. "You shore ain't no reg'lar hallucy-nation," he said. "I'm obliged to ya." Suddenly he laughed. "Jest imagine, thankin' a piece o' yor dee-lirium tremens fer givin' you yer hat back! Ah jest cain't figger out what's goin' on around here. Say! Are you real, or was that Injun real? 'Cause in case you ain't noticed, you're a danged sight bigger'n he is. You cain't both be real."

"I don't think you ought to worry about it. What's your name?"

The cowboy seemed embarrassed and hung his head. "M'name's Boone. But the fellas all call me Boohoo. That's on account of Ah cry so easy. It's m'soft heart. Show me some'n sad, or scare me just a little, and the tears jest come to mah eyes. Ah cain't help it."

Omri, who had been somewhat of a cry-baby himself until very recently, was not inclined to be scornful about this, and said, "That's okay. Only you needn't be scared of me. And as for the Indian, he's my friend and he won't hurt you, he's promised. Now I'd like you and your horse to go back into that big crate. I'll stick the knot back in the wood, you'll feel safer. Then I'll get you some breakfast." Boone brightened visibly at this. "What would you like?"

"Aw shucks, Ah ain't that hungry. Coupla bits o' steak and three or four eggs, sittin' on a small heap o'beans and washed down with a jug o' cawfee'll suit me just dandy."

"You'll be lucky," thought Omri.

Chapter Ten

BREAKFAST TRUCE

HE CREPT DOWNSTAIRS. The house was still asleep. He decided to cook breakfast for himself and his cowboy and Indian. He was quite a good cook, but he'd mostly done sweet stuff before; however, any fool, he felt sure, could fry an egg. The steaks were out of the question, but beans were no problem. Omri put frying-pan over gas and margarine in pan. The fat began to smoke. Omri broke an egg into it, or tried to, but the shell, instead of coming cleanly apart, crumpled up somehow in his hand and landed in the hot fat mixed up with the egg.

Hm. Not as easy as he'd thought. Leaving the mess to cook, shell and all, he got a tin of beans out of the cupboard and opened it without trouble. Then he got a saucepan and began pouring the beans in. Some of them got into the egg-pan somehow and seemed to explode. The egg was beginning to curl and the pan was still smoking. Alarmed, he turned off the gas. The centre of the egg still wasn't cooked and the beans in the pan were stone cold but the smell in the kitchen was beginning to worry him – he didn't want his mother coming down. He tipped the whole lot into a bowl, hacked a lopsided slice off the loaf, and tiptoed up the stairs again.

Little Bull was standing outside his longhouse with hands on hips, waiting for him.

"You bring food?" he asked in his usual bossy way.

"Yes."

"First, Little Bull want ride."

"First, you must eat while it's hot, I've been to a lot of trouble to cook it for you," Omri said, sounding like his mother.

Little Bull didn't know how to take this, so he burst into a rather forced laugh and pointed at him scornfully. "Omri cook – Omri woman!" he teased. But Omri wasn't bothered.

"All the best cooks are men," he retorted. "Come on, you're going to eat with Boone."

Little Bull's laughter died instantly.

"Who Boone?"

"You know who he is. The cowboy."

The Indian's hands came off his hips and one of them went for his knife.

"Oh, knock it off, Little Bull! Have a truce for breakfast, otherwise you won't get any."

Leaving him with that thought to chew over, Omri crossed to the crate, in which Boone was grooming his white horse with a wisp of cloth he'd found clinging to a splinter. He'd taken off the little saddle, but the bridle was still on.

"Boone! I've brought something to eat," said Omri.

"Yup. Ah thought Ah smelt some'n good," said Boone. "Let's git to it."

Omri put his hand down. "Climb on."

"Ah, shucks – where'm Ah goin'? Why cain't Ah eat in mah box, where it's safe?" whined Boone. But he clambered up into Omri's palm and sat grumpily with his back against his middle finger.

"You're going to eat with the Indian," said Omri.

Boone leapt up so suddenly he nearly fell off, and had to grab hold of a thumb to steady himself.

"Hell, no, Ah ain't!" he yelled. "You just put me down, son, ya hear? I ain't sharin' m'vittles with no lousy scalp-snafflin' Injun and that's m'last word!" It was, as it happened, his last word before being set down within a few centimetres of his enemy on the seed-tray.

They both bent their legs into crouches, as if uncertain whether to leap at each other's throats or turn and flee. Omri hurriedly spooned up some egg and beans and held it between them.

"Smell that!" he ordered them. "Now you eat together or you don't get any at all, so make up your minds to it. You can start fighting again afterwards if you must."

He took a bit of clean paper and laid it, like a table cloth, under the spoon. Then he broke off some crumbs of bread crust and pushed a little into each of their hands. Still with their eyes fixed on each other's faces, Indian and cowboy sidled towards the big, steaming 'bowl' of food from opposite sides. Little Bull, after hesitating, was first to shoot his arm out and dip the bread into the egg. The sudden movement startled Boone so much he let out a yell and tried to run, but Omri's hand was blocking the way.

"Don't be silly, Boone," he said firmly.

"Ah ain't bein' silly! Them Injuns ain't jest ornery and savage. Them's *dirty*. And Ah ain't eatin' from the same bowl as no—"

"Boone," said Omri quietly. "Little Bull is no dirtier than you. You should see your own face."

"Is that mah fault? What kinda hallucy-nation are ya, anyways, tellin' me Ah'm dirty when ya didn't bring me no washin' water?"

This was a fair complaint, but Omri wasn't about to lose the argument on a side issue.

"You can have some after breakfast. But if you don't agree to eat with my Indian, I'm going to tell him your nickname."

The cowboy's face fell. "Now that ain't fair. That plumb ain't no ways fair," he muttered. But hunger was getting the better of him anyway, so, grumbling and swearing under his breath, he turned back and marched to his side of the spoon. By this time Little Bull was seated cross-legged on the piece of paper, a hunk of bean in one hand and a mess of egg in the other, eating heartily. Seeing this, Boone lost no time in tucking in, eyeing the Indian, who ignored him.

"Whur's muh cawfee?" he complained after he'd eaten a few bites. "Ah cain't start the day till Ah've had muh jug o' cawfee!"

Omri had completely forgotten about coffee, but he was beginning to be pretty well fed up with being bossed around by ungrateful little men, so he settled down to eat the remains of the food and simply said, "Well, you'll have to start this one without any."

Little Bull finished his breakfast and stood up.

"Now we fight," he announced, and reached for his knife.

Omri expected Boone to leap up and run, but he didn't. He just sat there munching bread and beans.

"Ah ain't finished yit," he said. "Ain't gonna fight till Ah'm plumb full o'vittles. So you kin jest sit down and wait, Redskin."

Omri laughed. "Good for you, Boone! Take it easy, Little Bull. Don't forget your promise."

Little Bull scowled. But he sat down again.

Boone ate and ate. It was hard not to suspect, after a while, that he was eating as much and as slowly as possible, to put off the moment when he would have to fight.

At last, very reluctantly, he scraped the last bit of egg from the spoon, wiped his hands on the side of his trousers, and stood up. Little Bull was on his feet instantly. Omri stood ready to part them.

"Looka here, Injun," said Boone. "If we're gonna fight, we're gonna fight fair. Probably ain't even a word for 'fair' in your language, but Ah'm here to tell ya, with me it's fight fair or don't fight a-tall."

"Little Bull fight fair, kill fair, scalp fair."

"You ain't gonna scalp nobody. Less'n ya take it off with yer teeth."

For answer, Little Bull raised his knife, which flashed in the morning light. Omri, his hands on his knees, waited.

"Yeah, Ah see it. But you ain't gonna have it much

longer. And why aincha? Because Ah ain't got one. Ah only got m'gun, and m'gun's run plumb outa bullets. What Ah got, and all Ah got, is m'fists. Oh — and one other thing. Ah got mah hallucy-nation here." He waved a hand at Omri without taking his eyes off Little Bull for a second. "And Ah know he don't want to see this here purty red scalp o'mine hangin' from no stinkin' redskin's belt. So if Ah fight, it's gonna be fist to fist, face to face — man to man, Injun! D'ja hear me? No weapons! Jest us two, and let's see if a white man cain't lick a red man in a fair fight. Less'n mebbe — jest mebbe — you ain't red a-tall, but yeller?" And Boone stepped round the bowl of the spoon, threw his empty gun on the ground, and put up his fists like a boxer.

Little Bull was nonplussed. He lowered his knife and stared at Boone. Whether Little Bull had completely understood the cowboy's strange speech was doubtful, but he couldn't mistake the gesture of throwing the gun away. As Boone began to dance round him, fists up, making little mock jabs towards his face, Little Bull was getting madder and madder. He made a sudden swipe at him with his knife. Boone jumped back.

"Oh, you naughty Injun! Ah see Ah'll have to set mah hallucy-nation on to you!"

But Omri didn't have to do anything. Little Bull had got the message. Throwing down the knife in a fury, he hurled himself on to Boone.

What followed was not a fist fight, or a wrestling match, or anything so well organized. It was just an all-in, no-holds-barred two-man war. They rolled on the ground pummelling, kicking and butting with their heads. At one point Omri thought he saw Boone trying to bite. Maybe he succeeded, because Little Bull suddenly let him go and Boone rolled away swift as a barrel down a slope and on to his legs and then, with a spring, like a bow-legged panther on to the Indian again. Feet first.

Little Bull let out a noise like "OOOF!" – caught Boone by both ankles, and heaved him off. Little Bull picked up a clod of compost and flung it after him, catching him full in the face. Then Little Bull got up and ran at him, holding both fists together and swinging them as he had swung the battle-axe. They caught the cowboy a heavy whack on the ear which sent him flying to one side. But as he flew, he caught Little Bull a blow in the chest with one boot. That left them both on the ground.

The next moment each of the men found himself pinned down by a giant finger.

"All right, boys. That's enough," said Omri, in his father's firm end-of-the-fight voice. "It's a draw. Now you must get cleaned up for school."

Chapter Eleven

SCHOOL

HE BROUGHT THEM a low type of egg-cup full of hot water and a corner of soap cut off a big cake, to wash with. They stood one on each side of it. Little Bull, already naked to the waist, lost no time in plunging his arms in and began energetically rubbing the whole of the top part of his body with his wet hands, throwing water everywhere. He made a lot of noise about it and seemed to be enjoying himself, though he ignored the soap.

Boone was a different matter. Omri had already noticed that Boone was none too fussy about being clean, and in fact didn't look as if he'd washed or shaved for weeks. Now he approached the hot water gingerly, eyeing Omri as if to see how little washing he could actually get away with.

"Come on, Boone! Off with that shirt, you can't wash your neck with a shirt on," said Omri briskly, echoing his mother.

With extreme reluctance, shivering theatrically, Boone dragged off his plaid shirt, keeping his hat on.

"I should think your hair could do with a wash too," said Omri.

Boone stared at him.

"Wash mah *hair*?" he asked incredulously. "Washin' hair's fur *wimmin*, 'tain't fer men!" But he did consent to rub his hands lightly over the piece of soap, although grimacing hideously as if it were some slimy dead thing. Then he rinsed them hastily, smeared some water on his face, and reached for his shirt without even drying himself.

"Boone!" said Omri sternly. "Just look at Little Bull! You called him dirty, but at least he's washing himself thoroughly! Now you just do something about your neck and — well, under your arms."

Boone's look was now one of stark horror.

"Under mah arms!"

"*And* your chest I should think. I'm not taking you to school all sweaty."

"Hell! Don't you go runnin' down sweat! It's sweat that keeps a man clean!"

After a lot of bullying, Omri managed to get him to wash at least a few more bits of himself.

"You'll have to wash your clothes some time, too," he said.

But this was too much for Boone.

"Ain't nobody gonna touch muh duds, and that's final," he said. "Ain't bin washed since ah bought 'em. Water takes all the stuffin' outa good cloth. Without all the dust 'n' sweat they don't keep ya warm no more."

At last they were ready, and Omri pocketed them and ran down to breakfast. He felt tense with excitement. He'd never carried them around the house before. It was risky, but not so risky as taking them to school — he felt that having family breakfast with them secretly in his pocket was like a training for taking them to school.

Breakfast in his house was often a dicey meal anyway, with everybody more or less bad-tempered. Today, for instance, Adiel had lost his football shorts and was blaming everybody in turn, and their mother had just discovered that Gillon, contrary to his assurances the night before when he had wanted to watch television, had not finished his homework. Their father was grumpy because he had wanted to do some gardening and it was raining yet again.

"I *know* I put them in the laundry basket," Adiel was saying fretfully.

"If you did, I washed them, in which case they're back in your top drawer," said his mother. "But you didn't, because I didn't, and they're not! Now listen to me, Gillon—"

"It's only a tiny bit of history, one mini little castle to draw and a mouldy paragraph on mottes and bailies to write," said Gillon. "I can do it at school."

"Stinking climate," muttered their father. "Those onion sets will rot if I don't get them in soon."

"Gillon, did you borrow them?" put in Adiel.

"I've got my own."

"You actually told me a lie last night—" said his mother.

"I did not! I said I'd *nearly* finished."

"There was no mention of 'nearly'!"

"You probably didn't hear."

"Probably not," retorted their mother. "With the row going on from *The Water Margin*."

Omri ate his cereal in silence, grinning to himself, hugging his secret. He slipped a couple of cornflakes in his pockets.

"I bet Omri took them!" said Adiel suddenly.

Omri looked up. "Took what?"

"My *shorts*."

"What on earth would I want your shorts for?"

"It might be your idea of a joke to hide them," Adiel retorted.

This was not as outrageous as it sounds. It had, until very recently, been a common form of revenge, when Adiel or Gillon had been specially unbearable, for Omri to sneak some valuable possession and hide it.

Now, however, Omri felt very far away from such babyishness, and was quite insulted.

"Don't be stupid," he said.

"So you did," said Adiel in triumph.

"I did not!"

"You're red in the face — that's proof you're guilty!"

"I swear!" said Omri.

"They're probably under your bed," said their mother to Adiel. "Go up and have a look."

"I have looked! I've looked everywhere."

"Oh, my God, it's starting to hail now," said their father despairingly. "So much for the apple blossom."

Under cover of the moans that went up about the prospect of no apples in the autumn, and the exclamations about the size of the hailstones, Omri slipped his coat on and ran through the bouncing ice-lumps to school. On the way he stopped under a protecting yew tree and took the little men out. He showed them each a large hailstone, which, to them, was the size of a football.

"Now, when we get to school," said Omri, "you must lie very still and quiet in my pockets. I'm putting you in separate ones because I can't risk any fighting or quarrelling. If you're seen I don't know what will happen."

"Danger?" asked Little Bull, his eyes gleaming.

"Yes. Not of death so much. You might be taken away

from me. Then you'd never get back to your own time."

"You mean we'd never wake up outa this here drunken dream," said Boone.

But Little Bull was staring at him very thoughtfully. "Own time," he said musingly. "Very strange magic."

Omri had never arrived at school with more apprehension in his heart, not even on spelling-test days. And yet he was excited too. Once he had taken a white mouse to school in his blazer pocket. He'd planned to do all sorts of fiendish things with it, like putting it up his teacher's trouser leg (he had had a man teacher then) or down the back of a girl's neck, or just putting it on the floor and letting it run around and throw the whole class into chaos. (He hadn't actually dared do anything with it except let it peep out and make his neighbours giggle.) This time he had no such plans. All he was hoping was that he could get through the day without anybody finding out what he had in his pockets.

Patrick was waiting for him at the school gate.

"Have you got him?"

"Yes."

His eyes lit up. "Give! I want him."

"All right," said Omri. "But you have to promise that you won't show him to *anybody*."

Omri reached into his right-hand pocket, closed his fingers gently round Boone, and passed him into Patrick's hand.

The moment he'd let go of him, things started to happen.

A particularly nasty little girl called April, who had been playing across the playground at the moment of the transaction, was at Patrick's side about two seconds later.

"What've you got there then, what did he give you?" she asked in her raucous voice like a crow's.

Patrick flushed red. "Nothing! Push off!" he said.

At once April pointed her witchy finger at him. "Look at Patrick blu-shing, look at Patrick blu-shing!" she squawked. Several other children speedily arrived on the scene and soon Patrick and Omri found themselves surrounded.

"What's he got? Bet it's something horrid!"

"Bet it's a slimy toad!"

"A little wriggly worm, more like."

"A beetle!"

"Like him!"

Omri felt his blood begin to get hot in his head. He longed to bash them all one by one, or better still, all at once – Bruce Lee, knocking down hordes of enemies like skittles. He imagined them all rolling backwards down a long wide flight of steps, in waves, bowled over by his flashing fist and flying feet.

The best he could manage in reality, though, was to lower his head and, keeping his hand cupped stiffly over his left pocket, barge through the chanting circle. He caught one of them a good butt in the stomach which was rather satisfying. Patrick was hot on his heels, and they belted across the playground and in through the double doors, which fortunately had just been opened.

Once inside, they were relatively safe. There were teachers all over the place, and any kind of fighting or taunting, above a sly pinch or a snide whisper, was out. Patrick and Omri slowed to a walk, went to their places and sat down, trying to look perfectly calm and ordinary so as not to attract their teacher's attention. Their breathing gave them away, though.

"Well, you two, what are you puffing about? Been running?"

They glanced at each other and nodded.

"So long as you've not been fighting," she said, giving them a sharp look. She always behaved as if a little fight was a long step along the road to hell.

Neither of the boys got much work done during the morning. They couldn't concentrate. Each of them was too aware of the passenger in his pocket. Both Little Bull and Boone were restless, particularly Little Bull. Boone was naturally lazier; he kept dozing off in the dark, and then waking with a little jump that made Patrick very nervous. But Little Bull was scrambling about the whole time.

It was during the third period — when they were all in the main hall listening to the headmaster, whose name was

Mr Johnson, announcing plans for the end-of-year show — that Little Bull got really sick and tired of being imprisoned, and started to take drastic action.

The first thing Omri knew was a sharp prick in his hip, as if an insect had stung him. For a moment he was silly enough to think an ant or even a wasp had somehow got into his clothes, and he only just stopped himself from slapping his hand instinctively against his side to squash it. Then there came another jab, sharper than the first, sharp enough in fact to make Omri let out a short yelp.

"Who did that?" asked Mr Johnson irritably.

Omri didn't answer, but the girls sitting near him began giggling and staring.

"Was that you, Omri?"

"Yes. I'm sorry, something stuck into me."

"Patrick! Did you stick a pencil into Omri?" (Such a thing was not unknown during assemblies when they were bored.)

"No Mr Johnson."

"Well, be quiet when I'm talking!"

Another jab, and this time Little Bull meant business and kept his knife embedded. Omri shouted "Ouch!" and jumped to his feet.

"Omri! Patrick! Leave the hall!"

"But I didn't—" began Patrick.

"Out, I said!" shouted Mr Johnson furiously.

They left, Patrick walking normally and Omri dancing about like a flea on a hot stove, shouting "Ow! OW!" at every step as Little Bull continued to dig the needle-point of his knife in. The whole school was in hysterics of laughter (and Mr Johnson was frothing with rage) by the time they reached the swing-doors and departed.

Outside, they ran (well, Patrick ran and Omri performed a series of sideways leaps) to the far end of the playground. On the way Omri plunged his hand into his pocket, seized Little Bull, and dragged him out. The agony stopped.

Safe in a sheltered corner behind some privet bushes Omri held his persecutor at eye-level and shook him violently, the way you shake a bottle of medicine. He called him the worst names he could possibly think of. When he'd run out of swear-words (which was not for some time) he hissed, like Mr Johnson, "What do you mean by it? How dare you? How dare you stick your knife into me?"

"Little Bull dare! Omri keep in dark many hours! Little Bull want see school place, not lie in hot dark! No breathe, no see! Want *enjoy!*"

"I warned you you wouldn't, it's not my fault you made me bring you! Now you've got me into trouble."

Little Bull looked mulish, but he stopped shouting. Seeing this evidence that a truce was on its way, Omri calmed down a bit too.

"Listen. I can't let you see because I can't take you out. You have no idea what would happen if I did. If any of the other children saw you they'd want to grab you and mess you about – you'd hate it, and it would be terribly dangerous too, you'd probably get hurt or killed. You've *got* to lie quiet till school's over. I'm sorry if you're bored but it's your own fault."

Little Bull thought this over and then he said a most astonishing thing.

"Want Boone."

"What? Your enemy?"

"Better enemy than alone in dark."

Patrick had taken Boone out of his pocket. The little cowboy was sitting on his hand. They were gazing at each other. Omri said, "Boone, Little Bull says he wants you. He's lonely and bored."

"Well, ain't that jest too bad!" said Boone sarcastically. "After he tried to kill me, now he's come over all lovey-dovey. Listen, you redskin!" he shouted through cupped hands across the yawning gulf between Patrick and Omri. "I don't care how lonesome y'are! Ah don't care if'n ya drop down daid! Th'only good Injun's a daid Injun, d'ya hear me?"

Little Bull turned his head haughtily away.

"I think he's lonely too, really," said Patrick in a whisper. "He's been crying."

"Oh no, not again!" said Omri. "Honestly, Boone — at your age—"

Just then they heard their teacher calling them from the school door.

"Come on, you two! You've not got the day off, you know!"

"Give me your knife," said Omri to Little Bull on a sudden impulse. "Then I'll put you together." With only a moment's hesitation, Little Bull handed over his knife. Omri slipped it into the small breast-pocket of his shirt which was empty and where it wouldn't easily get lost. Then he said to Patrick, "Let me have Boone."

"No!"

"Just for the next lesson. Then at lunchtime you can have both of them. They'll keep each other company. They can't do each other much damage in a pocket."

Reluctantly Patrick handed Boone over. Omri held them one in each hand so they were face to face.

"Be good, you two. Try talking to each other instead of fighting. But whatever you do, don't make any noise." And he slipped them both into his left-hand pocket and he and Patrick ran back to the school buildings.

Chapter Twelve

TROUBLE WITH AUTHORITY

WHAT WAS LEFT of the morning passed uneventfully. Omri even got a few sums done. By the time the first whiffs of school dinner were beginning to flood through the classrooms, Omri was congratulating himself on a stroke of genius in putting the two little men together. There had not been another peep out of either of them, and when Omri took an opportunity (when the teacher's back was turned) to open his pocket stealthily and peer down into it, he was pleased to see them, sitting in the bottom of it, face to face, apparently having a conversation. They were both gesticulating with their arms – there was too much noise all round for Omri to be able to hear their tiny voices.

He had given some thought to the matter of their dinner. He would separate them for that, one into each pocket and slip some dry bits of food down to them. Omri let himself play with the wonderful fantasy of what the other kids' reaction would be if he casually brought them out and sat them on the edge of his plate… Funny to think that he would certainly have done it, only a week ago, without thinking about the dangers.

The bell rang at last. There was the usual stampede, and Omri found himself in the queue next to Patrick.

"Come on then, hand them over," Patrick whispered over his tray as they shuffled towards the fragrant hatches.

"Not *now*, everyone'd see."

"You said at lunchtime."

"After lunch."

"Now. I want to feed them."

"Well, you can have Boone, but I want to feed Little Bull."

"You said I could have them both!" said Patrick, no longer in a whisper. Others in the queue began to turn their heads.

"Will you shut up?" hissed Omri.

"No," said Patrick in a loud clear voice. He held out his hand.

Omri felt trapped and furious. He looked into Patrick's eyes and saw what happens even to the nicest people when they want something badly and are determined to get it, come what may. Omri slammed his empty tray down on the floor and, taking Patrick by the wrist, pulled him out of the queue and into a quiet corner of the hall.

"Listen to me," he grated out between teeth clenched in anger. "If you let anything happen to Little Bull, I will bash you so hard your teeth will fall out." (This, of course, is the sort of thing that happens even to the nicest people when they are in a trap.) With that, he groped in his pocket and brought the two little men out. He didn't look at them or say goodbye to them. He just put them carefully into Patrick's hand and walked away.

He had lost his appetite, so he didn't get back in the queue; but Patrick did. He even pushed a bit, he was so eager to get some food to give to the cowboy and the Indian. Omri watched from a distance. He wished now he hadn't been too angry to give Patrick some pretty clear instructions. Like telling him to separate them. Now he thought about it, perhaps it wasn't a good idea to feed them in a pocket. Who wants to eat something that's descended between two layers of cloth and collected bits of dust and fluff? If he'd still had them, he would have taken them to some private place and taken them out to eat properly. Why had he ever brought them to school at all? The dangers here were too awful.

Watching, he suddenly stiffened. Patrick had reached the hatch now, and received his dinner. He almost ran with it to a table – he did try to go to one in the outside row near the windows, but a dinner-lady stopped him and made him sit in the middle of the hall. There were children all round him and on either side. Surely, thought Omri, surely he wasn't going to try to feed them there?

He saw Patrick take a pinch of bread and slip it into his pocket. He wasn't wearing a jacket; the men were in his jeans pocket. Fortunately the jeans were new and loose, but still he had to half stand up to get the bit of bread in; when he was sitting down the people in his pocket must be pretty well squashed against his leg. Omri imagined them trying to eat, held down flat by two thick layers of cloth. He could almost see Patrick imagining it, too. He was frowning uneasily and shifting around in his chair. The girl next to him spoke to him. She was probably telling him not to wriggle. Patrick said something sharp in reply. Omri sucked in his breath. If only Patrick wouldn't draw attention to himself!

Suddenly he gasped. The girl had given Patrick a hard push. He pushed her back. She nearly went off her chair. She stood up and pushed him with all her might, using both hands. He went flying over backwards, half on to the boy on the other side of him, who jumped from his place, spilling part of his dinner. Patrick landed on the floor.

Omri didn't stop to think. He raced towards him across the hall, dodging in and out among the tables. His heart was hammering with terror. If Patrick had fallen on them! Omri had a terrible, fleeting vision of the pocket of Patrick's jeans, with bloodstains spreading — he clamped down on his imagination.

By the time he got there, Patrick was back on his feet, but now the other boy was angry and clearly looking for a fight. The girl on his other side looked ready to clobber him too. Omri pushed between them, but a stout dinner lady was ahead of him.

"'Ere, 'ere, what's goin' on?" she asked, barging in with her big stomach and sturdy arms. She grabbed Patrick in one hand and the boy with the other and kind of dangled them at arm's length and shook them. "No fighting in 'ere, thank you very much, or it'll be off to the 'ead master's orfice before you can say knife, the 'ole bloomin' pack of you!" She dumped them down in their separate chairs as if they'd been bags of shopping. They were both thoroughly tousled and red-faced. Omri's eyes shot down to Patrick's thigh. No blood. No movement either, but at least no blood.

Everyone began to eat again as the stout dinner-lady stamped away, tut-tutting as she went. Omri leant over the back of Patrick's chair and whispered out of a dry mouth, "Are they all right?"

"How do I know," said Patrick sulkily. But his hand crept down and delicately explored the slight bump on the top of his leg where his pocket was. Omri held his breath. "Yeah, they're okay. They're moving," he muttered.

Omri went out into the playground. He felt too jumpy to stay indoors, or eat, or anything. How would he get them back from Patrick, who, quite obviously, was not a fit person to have charge of them? Nice as he was, as a friend, he just wasn't fit. It must be because he didn't take them seriously yet. He simply didn't seem to realize that they were *people*.

When the bell rang Omri still hadn't come to any decision. He hurried back into school. Patrick was nowhere to be seen. Omri looked round for him frantically. Maybe he'd gone into the washroom to be private and give the men something to eat. Omri went in there and called him softly, but there was no answer. He returned to his place in the classroom. There was no sign of Patrick. And there was no further sign of him till about halfway through the lesson – not one word of which Omri took in, he was so worried.

At last, when the teacher turned her back to write on the board, Patrick slipped round a partition, rushed across the room silently and dropped into his chair.

"Where the *hell* have you been?" asked Omri under his breath.

"In the music-room," said Patrick smugly. The music-room was not a room at all, but a little alcove off the gym in which the musical instruments were stored, together with some of the bulkier apparatus like the jumping horse. "I sat under the horse and fed them," he muttered out of the side of his mouth. "Only they weren't very hungry."

"I bet they weren't!" said Omri, "after all they'd been through!"

"Cowboys and Indians are used to rough treatment," Patrick retorted. "Anyway, I left some food in my pocket for later if they want it."

"It'll get all squashy."

"Oh, so what? Don't fuss so much, they don't mind!"

"How do you know what they mind?" said Omri hotly, forgetting to whisper. The teacher turned round.

"Oh ho, so there you are, Patrick! And where have you been, may I enquire?"

"Sorry, Miss Hilton."

"I didn't ask if you were sorry. I asked where you'd been."

Patrick coughed and lowered his head. "In the wash-room," he mumbled.

"For nearly twenty minutes? I don't believe you! Are you telling me the truth?" Patrick mumbled something. "Patrick, answer me. Or I'll send you to the headmaster."

This was the ultimate threat. The headmaster was very fierce and could make you feel five centimetres high. So

Patrick said, "I was in the music-room, and that's true. And I forgot the time."

And that's not true, added Omri silently. Miss Hilton was nobody's fool. She knew it too.

"You'd better go and see Mr Johnson," she said. "Omri, you go too, chattering away there as usual. Tell him I said you were both disturbing the class and that I'm tired of it."

They got up silently and walked through the tables, while all the girls giggled and the boys smirked or looked sorry for them, according to whether they liked them or not. Omri glanced at Patrick under his eyebrows. They were for it now.

Outside the headmaster's office they stopped.

"You knock," whispered Omri.

"No, you," retorted Patrick.

They dithered about for a few minutes, but it was useless to put it off, so in the end they both knocked together.

"Yes?" came a rather irritable voice from inside.

They edged round the door. Mr Johnson was seated at his large desk, working at some papers. He looked up at once.

"Well, you two? What was it this time – fighting in the playground or talking in class?"

"Talking," they said, and Patrick added, "And I was late."

"Why?"

"I just was."

"Oh, don't waste my time!" snapped Mr Johnson. "There must have been a reason."

"I was in the music-room, and I forgot the time," Patrick repeated.

"I don't remember you being especially musical. What were you doing in the music-room?"

"Playing."

"Which instrument?" asked Mr Johnson with a touch of sarcasm.

"Just – playing."

"*With what?*" he asked, raising his voice.

"With a – with—" he glanced at Omri. Omri threw him a warning grimace.

"What are you pulling faces about, Omri? You look as if someone's just stuck a knife into you."

Omri started to giggle, and that set Patrick off.

"Somebody just did!" spluttered Patrick.

Mr Johnson was in no such jolly mood, however. He was scowling horribly.

"What are you talking about, you silly boy? Stop that idiotic noise!"

Patrick's giggles were getting worse. If they hadn't been where they were, Omri thought, Patrick would have folded up completely.

"Someone – did – stick a knife into him!" hiccupped

Patrick, and added, "A very small one!" His voice went off into a sort of whinny.

Omri had stopped giggling and was staring in awful anticipation at Patrick. When Patrick got into this state he was apt to do and say anything, like someone who's drunk. He took hold of his arm and gave it a sharp shake.

"Shut up!" he hissed.

Mr Johnson got up slowly and came round his desk. Both boys fell back a step, but Patrick didn't stop giggling. On the contrary, it got worse. He seemed to be getting completely helpless. Mr Johnson loomed over him and took him by the shoulder.

"Listen here, my lad," he said in fearsome tones. "I want you to pull yourself together this moment and tell me what you meant. If there is any child in this school who so far forgets himself as to stick knives into people, or even pretend to, I want to know about it! Now, who was it?"

"Little – Bull!" Patrick squeaked out. Tears were running down his cheeks.

Omri gasped. "Don't!"

"Who?" asked Mr Johnson, puzzled.

Patrick didn't answer. He couldn't. He was now speechless with nervous, almost hysterical laughter.

Mr Johnson gave him a shake of his own that rocked him back and forth on his feet like one of those weighted dolls that won't fall down. Then, abruptly, he let him go and strode back to his desk.

"You seem to be quite beyond yourself," he said sharply. "I think the only thing I can do is telephone your father."

Patrick stopped laughing instantly.

"Ah, that's better!" said Mr Johnson. "Now. Who did you say had stabbed Omri?"

Patrick stood rigid, like a soldier at attention. He didn't look at Omri, he just stared straight at Mr Johnson.

"I want the truth, Patrick, and I want it now!"

"Little Bull," said Patrick very clearly and much louder than necessary.

"Little Who?"

"Bull."

Mr Johnson looked blank, as well he might. "Is that somebody's nickname, or is this your idea of a joke?"

Patrick gave his head one stiff shake. Omri was staring at him, as if paralysed. Was he going to tell? He knew Patrick was afraid of his father.

"Patrick. I shall ask you once more. Who is this – Little Bull?"

Patrick opened his mouth. Omri clenched his teeth. He was helpless. Patrick said, "He's an Indian."

"A what?" asked Mr Johnson. His voice was very quiet now. He didn't sound annoyed any more.

"An Indian."

Mr Johnson looked at him steadily for some seconds, his chin resting on his hand.

"You are too old to tell those sort of lies," he said quietly.

"It's not a lie!" Patrick shouted suddenly, making both Omri and Mr Johnson jump. "It's not a lie! He's a real live Indian!"

To Omri's utter horror, he saw that Patrick was beginning to cry. Mr Johnson saw it too. He was not an unkind man. No headmaster is much good if he can't scare the wits out of children when necessary, but Mr Johnson didn't enjoy making them cry.

"Now then, Patrick, none of that," he said gruffly. But Patrick misunderstood. He thought he was still saying he didn't believe him.

He now said the words Omri had been dreading most.

"It's true and I can prove it!"

And his hand went to his pocket.

Omri did the only thing possible. He jumped at him and knocked him over. He sat on his chest and pinned his hands to the ground.

"You dare – you dare – you dare—" he ground out between clenched teeth before Mr Johnson managed to drag him off.

"Get out of the room!" he roared.

"I won't!" Omri choked out. He'd be crying himself in a minute, he felt so desperate.

"OUT!"

Omri felt his collar seized. He was almost hiked off his feet. The next thing he knew, he was outside the door and hearing the key turning.

Without stopping to think, Omri hurled himself against the door, kicking and banging with his fists.

"Don't show him, Patrick, don't show him! Patrick, don't, I'll kill you if you show him!" he screamed at the top of his lungs.

Footsteps came running. Through his tears and a sort of red haze, Omri just about saw Mrs Hunt, the headmaster's elderly secretary, bearing down on him. He got in a couple more good kicks and shouts before she had hold of him and, with both arms round his waist, carried him, shrieking and struggling, bodily into her own little office.

The minute she put him down he tried to bolt, but she hung on.

"Omri! Omri! Stop it, calm down, whatever's come over you, you naughty boy!"

"Please don't let him! Go in and stop him!" Omri cried.

"Who? What?"

Before Omri could explain he heard the sound of footsteps from the next room. Suddenly Mr Johnson appeared, holding Patrick by the elbow. The headmaster's face was dead white, and his mouth was partly open. Patrick's head was hung down and his shoulders were heaving with sobs. One look at him told Omri the worst. Patrick had shown the headmaster.

Chapter Thirteen

ART AND ACCUSATION

MR JOHNSON OPENED and shut his mouth for several seconds without a sound coming out. At last he croaked: "Mrs Hunt… I'm afraid I'm unwell… I'm going home to bed… Will you take charge of this child…" His voice dropped to a mumble like an old man's. Omri just caught the words, "… back to their lessons…" Then Mr Johnson let go of Patrick's arm, turned, walked most unsteadily to the door, and then put his hand on it and swayed as if he might fall over.

"Mr Johnson!" said Mrs Hunt in a shocked tone. "Shall I call a taxi?"

"No… No… I'll be all right," And the headmaster, without looking back, tottered out into the corridor.

"Well!" exclaimed Mrs Hunt. "What*ever* have you been doing to the poor man?"

Neither of them answered. Omri was staring at Patrick, or rather, at his pocket. Patrick's shoulders were heaving and he was not looking at anybody. Mrs Hunt was obviously flummoxed.

"Well. You'd better go to the wash-room and wash your faces, both of you, and then go back to your classroom as fast as you can toddle," she said in her funny old-fashioned way. "Run along!"

They needed no second telling. Neither of them said a word until they were in the boys' wash-room. Patrick went straight to a basin and began running the cold water. He splashed some on to his face, getting his collar soaked. Omri stood watching him. Obviously he was as upset as Omri, if not more so. Once again Omri felt their friendship trembling on the edge of destruction. He drew a deep breath.

"You showed him," he said at last in a trembling voice.

Patrick said nothing. He dried his face on the roller-towel. He was still gasping the way one does when one has been crying.

"Give them back to me. Both of them."

Patrick reached slowly into his pocket. He put his closed hand backwards. Omri looked as his fingers slowly opened.

Little Bull and Boone were sitting there, absolutely terrified. They were actually clinging to each other. Even Little Bull was hiding his face and they were both trembling.

With infinite slowness and care, so as not to frighten them more, Omri took them into his own hand. "It's all right," he whispered, bringing them near to his face. "Please. It's all right." Then he put them carefully in his pocket and said to Patrick in a low voice, "You bloody, stupid fool."

Patrick turned. His face gave Omri more of a jolt than Mr Johnson's had. It was white-mottled-red, with swollen eyes.

"I had to!" he said. "I had to! He'd have phoned my dad! They'd have made me tell in the end. Anyhow, he didn't believe in them. He thought he was seeing things. He just stood there, gaping at them. He didn't even touch them. When they moved he gave a yell and then I thought he was going to fall over. He went white as a ghost. You saw. He didn't believe his eyes, Omri, honest! He'll think he dreamt it!" Omri went on looking at him stonily. "Can't I – can't I have Boone?" asked Patrick in a small voice.

"No."

"Please! I'm sorry I told – I *had* to!"

"They're not safe with you. You *use* them. They're people. You can't use people."

Patrick didn't ask again. He gave one more hiccupping sob and went out.

Omri took the little men out of his pocket again and lifted them to his face. Boone was lying flat on his front, holding his big hat down over his ears as if trying to shut out the world. But Little Bull stood up.

"Big man shout. Give fear!" he said angrily. "Small ears – big noise – no good!"

"I know. I'm sorry," said Omri. "But it's okay now. I'm going to take you home."

"What about wife?"

His promise! Omri had forgotten all about that.

Another Indian! Another live little person to worry about... Omri had heard about people going grey-haired almost overnight if they had too much worry. He felt it might easily happen to him. He thought back to the time, only a few days ago, when this had all started and he had fondly imagined it was going to be the greatest fun anybody had ever had. Now he realized that it was more like a nightmare.

But Little Bull was looking at him challengingly. He *had* promised.

"Right after school," he said, "we'll go to the shop."

There was still another hour of lessons to be got through. Fortunately it was two periods of art. In the art-room you could go away into a corner and even sit with your back turned to the teacher if you liked. Omri went to the furthest and darkest corner.

"Omri, don't try to draw there," said the art teacher. "You're in your own light — it's bad for your eyes."

"I'm going to draw something huge anyway," said Omri.

All the others sat near the long windows. He was quite alone, and if the teacher approached him he would hear her feet on the bare floor. He suddenly felt he must — he simply *must* get a little fun out of this somehow. He cautiously fished Little Bull and Boone out of his pocket.

They stood on the sheet of white drawing paper as if on a stretch of snow, and looked about them.

"This school place?" asked Little Bull.

"Yes. Sshhh!"

"Sure don't look much like the school Ah went to!" exclaimed Boone. "Whar's the rows o' desks? Whar's the slate 'n' bit o' chalk? Why ain't the teacher talkin'?"

"We're doing art. We can sit where we like. She doesn't talk much, she just lets us get on with it," replied Omri in the softest whisper he could possibly manage.

"Art, eh?" asked Boone, brightening up. "Say, that wuz mah best subject! Ah wuz allus top in art, on'y thing Ah wuz any good at! Still draw a mite when Ah gits a chance, if'n ain't nobody around t'laugh at me." He reached into the pocket of his own tiny jeans and fished out a stub of pencil almost too small to see. "Kin Ah draw a mite on yor paper?" he asked.

Omri nodded. Boone strode to the very centre of the paper, looked all round at the white expanse stretching away from him in every direction, and gave a deep sigh of satisfaction. Then he knelt down and began to draw.

Little Bull and Omri watched. From the microscopic point of Boone's pencil there developed a most amazing scene. It was a prairie landscape, with hills and cacti and a few tufts of sage-brush. Boone sketched in, with sure strokes, some wooden buildings such as Omri had often seen on cowboy films – a saloon with a swinging sign reading 'Golden Dollar Saloon' in twirly writing; a post office and general store, a livery stable, and a stone house with a barred window and a sign saying 'Jail'. Then, moving swiftly on his knees, as it were from one end of his 'street' to another, Boone drew in the foreground – figures of men and women, wagons, horses, dogs, and all the trappings of a little town.

From Boone's point of view, he was drawing something quite large, making the best use of his vast piece of paper; but from Omri's, the drawing was minute, perfect in its detailing but smaller than any human hand could possibly have made it. He and Little Bull watched, fascinated.

"Boone, you're an artist!" Omri breathed at last, when Boone had even made the mud on the unpaved street look real. Little Bull grunted.

"But not like real place," he said.

Boone didn't trouble to answer, in fact he was so absorbed he probably didn't hear. But Omri frowned. Then he understood. Of course! Boone's town was part of an America which was not thought of during Little Bull's time.

"Boone," he whispered, bending his head down. "What year is it — your town — your time?"

"Last time Ah saw a newspaper it was 1889," said Boone. "There! That's muh drawin'. Not bad, huh?"

"It's absolutely brilliant," said Omri, enthralled.

"Omri!"

Omri jumped. His two hands instantly cupped themselves over the two men.

From the other side of the room, the teacher said, "I see it's no use trying to stop you chattering. You even do it when you're alone! Bring me your picture."

For a moment Omri hesitated. But it was too marvellous to be passed up! He scooped the men into his pocket and picked up the sheet of paper. For once he wouldn't stop to think. He'd just enjoy himself.

He carried Boone's drawing to the teacher and put it innocently into her hand.

What happened then made up for a good deal of the worry and general anxiety the little men had caused him.

First she just glanced. At a *glance*, the drawing in the middle of the paper just looked like a scribble or a smudge.

"I thought you said you were going to do something huge," she said with a laugh. "This isn't much more than a—"

And then she took a second, much closer, look.

She stared without speaking for about two minutes, while Omri felt inside him the beginnings of a huge, gleeful, uncontrollable laugh. Abruptly the teacher, who had been perched on a desk, stood up and went to a cupboard. Omri was not surprised when she turned round to see a magnifying glass in her hand.

She put the paper down on a table and bent over it, with the glass poised. She examined the drawing for several minutes more. Her face was something to see! Some of the nearest children had become aware that something unusual was going on, and were also craning to see what the teacher was looking at so attentively. Omri stood with the same innocent look on his face, waiting, the laugh slowly rising inside him. Fun? This *was* fun, if you liked! *This* was what he'd been imagining!

The teacher looked at him. Her face was not quite as stunned as Mr Johnson's had been, but it was an absolute picture of bafflement.

"Omri," she said. "How in the name of all that's holy did you *do* this?"

"I like drawing small," said Omri quite truthfully.

"*Small!* This isn't small! It's tiny! It's infinitesimal! It's microscopic!" Her voice was rising higher with every word. Several of the other children had now stood up and were crowding round the paper, peering at it in absolute stupefaction. Small gasps and exclamations of wonder were rising on all sides. Omri's held-in laugh threatened to explode.

The teacher's eyes were now narrow with astonishment – and doubt.

"Show me," she said, "the pencil you used."

This took Omri aback, but only for a second.

"I left it over there. I'll just go and get it," he said sweetly.

He walked back to his table, his hand in his pocket. With his back turned he bent over, apparently searching the top of the table. Then he turned round, smiling, holding something cupped in his hand. He walked back.

"Here it is," he said, and held out his hand.

Everyone bent forward. The art teacher took hold of his hand and pulled it towards her. "Are you having me on, Omri? There's nothing there!"

"Yes there is."

She peered close until he could feel her warm breath on his hand.

"Don't breathe hard," said Omri, his laugh now

trembling on his very lips. "You'll blow it away. Maybe you'd see it better through the magnifying glass," he added kindly.

Slowly she raised the glass into position. She looked through.

"Can I see? Is it there? Can I look?" clamoured the other children. All except Patrick. He was sitting by himself, not paying attention to the crowd around Omri.

The art teacher lowered the glass. Her eyes were dazed.

"I don't believe it."

"It's there."

"How did you pick it up?"

"Ah. Well, that's a bit of a secret method I have."

"Yes," she said. "Yes, it must be. And you wouldn't feel like telling us?"

"No," said Omri in a trembly voice. His laugh was on the very brink — it was going to burst out — "May I go to the loo?"

"Yes," she said in a dazed voice. "Go on."

He took the drawing back and tottered to the door. He managed to get outside before the laugh actually blew out. But it was so loud, so overpowering that he was obliged to go right out into the playground. There he sank on to a bench and laughed till he felt quite weak. Her face! He had never enjoyed anything so much in his whole life. It had been worth it.

The bell rang. School was over. Omri brought out the men and held them up.

"Guys," he said (after all, they were both Americans), "I enjoyed that. Thank you. Now we're going to the shop."

Omri ran all the way to Yapp's and was there before most other children had even left the school. In ten minutes the place would be full of them, buying crisps and sweets and toys and comics. Just now he had it to himself, and he had to make the most of the few minutes he had.

He went directly to the corner where the boxes of plastic figures were kept, and stood with his back to the main counter. He was still holding Little Bull and Boone in his hand, and he put them down among the figures in the cowboys-and-Indians box. He hadn't reckoned on Boone's sensitive nature, however.

"Holy catfish! Look at all them dead bodies!" he squeaked, hiding his eyes. "There musta bin a massacree!"

"Not dead," said Little Bull scornfully. "Plass-tick." He kicked a plastic cowboy aside. "Too many," he said to Omri. "You find women. I choose."

"You'll have to be quick," said Omri in a low voice. He was already rummaging through the box, picking out the Indian women. There were very few. Of the five he found, one was clearly old, and two had babies tied on their backs in parcels laced up like boots.

"You don't fancy one with a baby, I suppose?"

Little Bull gave him a look.

"No – I thought not," said Omri hastily. "Well, what about these?"

He stood the two other figures on the edge of the table. Little Bull jumped down and faced them. He looked carefully first at one, then at the other. They both looked the same to Omri, except that one had a yellow dress and the other a blue. Each had a black pigtail and a headband with a single feather, and moccasins on her feet.

Little Bull looked up. His face showed furious disappointment.

"No good," he said. "This one from own tribe – taboo. This one ugly. Chief must have beautiful wife!"

"But there aren't any others."

"Many, many plass-tick! You look good, find other!"

Omri rummaged frantically, right to the bottom of the box. Kids were beginning to come into the shop.

He had almost despaired when he saw her. She lay face down on the very bottom of the box, half-hidden by two cowboys on horses. He pulled her out. She was the same as the others (apparently) except that she wore a red dress. They obviously all came out of the same mould, because they were all in the same position, as if walking. If the others were ugly, so would this one be.

Without much hope, he set her before Little Bull.

He stood staring at her. The shop was getting busy now. At any moment somebody would come up behind him, wanting to buy a plastic figure.

"Well?" asked Omri impatiently.

For another five seconds Little Bull stared. Then, without speaking a word, he nodded his head.

Omri didn't wait for him to change his mind. He scooped him and Boone back into his pocket and, picking up the approved figure, made his way to the counter.

"Just this one, please," he said.

Mr Yapp was looking at him. A very odd look.

"Are you sure you only want the one?" he asked.

"Yes."

Mr Yapp took the plastic figure, dropped it into a bag, and gave it back to Omri.

"Ten pence."

Omri paid and left the shop. Suddenly he felt a hand on his shoulder. He spun round. It was Mr Yapp. The look on his face was now not odd at all, but red and angry.

"Now you can hand over the two you stole."

Omri stood aghast. "I didn't steal any!"

"Don't add lying to your faults, my lad! I watched you put them in your pocket — a cowboy and an Indian."

Omri's mouth hung open. He thought he was going to be sick.

"I didn't—" he tried to say, but no words came out.

"Turn out your pockets."

"They're mine!" Omri managed to gasp.

"A likely story! And I suppose you brought them out to help you choose the new one?"

"Yes!"

"Ha, ha, ha," said Mr Yapp heavily. "Come on, stop playing around. I lose hundreds of pounds' worth of stuff a year to you thieving kids. When I do catch one of you red-handed, I'm not likely to let it pass – I know your sort – if I let you off, you'd be boasting to your pals at school how easy it is to get away with it, and most likely back you'd come tomorrow for another pocketful!"

Omri was now fighting back tears. Quite a crowd had collected, much like the crowd in the art-room – some of the same people, even – but his feelings were no longer so pleasant. He wished he could die or disappear.

"It's no good trying to get round me by crying!" shouted Mr Yapp. "Give me them back – right now, or I'll call the police!"

All at once Patrick was beside him.

"They're his," he said. "I know they're his because he showed them to me at school. A cowboy with a white stetson hat and an Indian in a Chief's headdress. He told me he was coming to buy a new one. Omri wouldn't steal."

Mr Yapp let go of Omri and looked at Patrick. He knew Patrick quite well, because it happened that Patrick's brother had once been his paper-boy.

"Will you vouch for him, then?"

"Course I will!" said Patrick staunchly. "I'm telling you, I saw 'em both this afternoon."

But still the shopkeeper wasn't convinced. "Let's see if they fit your description," he said.

Omri, who had been staring at Patrick as at some miraculous deliverer, felt his stomach drop into his shoes once more. But then he had an idea.

He reached both hands into his pockets. Then he held out one hand slowly, still closed, and everyone looked at it, though it was actually empty. The other hand he lifted to his mouth as if to stifle a cough, and whispered into it, "Lie still! Don't move! *Plastic!*" Then he put both hands before him and opened them.

The men played along beautifully. There they lay, side by side, stiff and stark, as like lifeless plastic figures as could possibly be. In any case Omri was taking no chances. He gave Mr Yapp just long enough to see that they were dressed as Patrick had said before closing his fingers again.

Mr Yapp grunted.

"Those aren't from my shop anyhow," he said. "All my Indian Chiefs are sitting down, and that sort of cowboy is always on a horse. Well, I'm sorry, lad. You'll have to excuse me, but you must admit, it did look suspicious."

Omri managed a sickly smile. The crowd were melting away. Mr Yapp shuffled back into the shop. Omri and Patrick were left alone on the pavement.

"Thanks," said Omri. It came out as croaky as a frog.

"That's okay. Have a Toffo."

They had a Toffo each and walked along side by side. After a while Omri said, "A man's gotta chew what a man's gotta chew."

They gave each other a quick grin.

"Let's give them some."

They stopped, took the men out, and gave them each some bits of the chocolate covering on the Toffo.

"That's a reward," said Patrick, "for playing dead."

Little Bull then naturally demanded to know what it had all been about, and the boys explained as well as they could. Little Bull was quite intrigued.

"Man say that Omri steal Little Bull?"

"Yes."

"And Boone?"

Omri nodded.

"Omri fool to steal Boone!" roared Little Bull, laughing. Boone, stuffing himself with chocolate, gave him a dirty look.

"Where woman?" Little Bull asked eagerly.

"I've got her."

"When make real?"

"Tonight."

Patrick gave him a look of pure longing. But he didn't say anything. They walked along again. They were getting near Omri's house.

Omri was thinking. After a while he said, "Patrick, what about you staying the night?"

Patrick's face lit up like a bulb.

"Could I? And see—"

"Yes."

"Wow! Thanks!"

They ran the rest of the way home.

Chapter Fourteen

THE FATEFUL ARROW

OMRI'S BROTHERS WERE already sitting at the tea-table when the two boys rushed in.

"Hi! What's for tea?" Omri asked automatically.

Gillon and Adiel didn't answer. Adiel had a funny smirk on his face. Omri hardly noticed.

"Let's make a sandwich and eat it upstairs," he suggested to Patrick.

They slapped some peanut butter on bread, poured mugs of milk, and hurried up the stairs to Omri's room, whispering all the way.

"How long does it take?"

"Only a few minutes."

"Can I see her?"

"Wait till we get upstairs!"

Omri opened the door — and stopped dead.

The white medicine-cupboard was gone.

"Wh-where is it?" gasped Patrick.

Omri didn't say a word. He turned and rushed downstairs again, with Patrick behind him.

"Okay, where've you hidden it?" he shouted as soon as he burst into the kitchen.

"I don't know what you're referring to," said Adiel loftily.

"Yes you damn well do! You've nicked my cupboard!"

"And supposing I did. It was only to teach you a lesson. You're always nicking my things and hiding them. Now you'll see how funny it *isn't*."

"When did I last take anything of yours? Tell me one thing in the last *month*!"

"My football shorts," said Adiel promptly.

"I never touched your lousy shorts, I already swore I hadn't!"

"I had to miss games again today because I didn't have them, *and* I got a detention for it, so you can be grateful I'm only punishing you tit-for-tat and not bashing you in," said Adiel with maddening calm.

Omri felt so furious he even wondered, for a moment, whether it was worth bashing *Adiel* in. But Adiel was enormous and it was hopeless. So after gazing at him for another moment with hate-filled eyes, Omri turned and dashed upstairs again, almost falling over Patrick on the way.

"What'll you do?"

"Look for it, of course!"

He was turning Adiel's room upside down like a madman when Adiel, slowly mounting the stairs in the direction of his homework, heard the racket and came running.

He stood in the doorway looking at the shambles of pulled-out drawers, degutted cupboards and furniture pulled awry.

"You LITTLE SWINE!" he howled, and dived at Omri. Omri fell to the ground with Adiel on top.

"I'll tear everything – you've got to pieces – till you give it back to me!" he shouted in jerks as Adiel shook and pummelled him.

"Then cough up my shorts!"

"I HAVEN'T GOT YOUR BLOODY SHORTS!" screamed Omri.

"Are these them?" asked a small voice in the background.

Adiel and Omri stopped fighting, and Adiel, sitting astride, twisted his neck to see. Patrick was just lifting a crumpled navy-blue object from behind a radiator.

Omri felt the anger go out of Adiel.

"Oh… Yes. It is, as a matter of fact. How did they get

there…?" But Omri knew perfectly well how; Adiel had hung them there to dry and they'd dropped off backwards.

Adiel scrambled up looking distinctly sheepish. He even helped Omri to his feet.

"Well, but you have hidden things in the past," he mumbled. "How was I to know?"

"Can I have my cupboard now?"

"Yeah, it's up in the attic. I piled a whole lot of stuff on it."

Omri and Patrick took the stairs to the attic two at a time.

They found the cupboard quite quickly, under a heap of bits and pieces. But Omri had carried it down to his room again before he made the fatal discovery.

"The key!"

The little twisted key with its red satin ribbon was missing.

Once again Omri ran into Adiel's room, to find Adiel uncomplainingly putting things straight.

"What happened to the key?"

"What key?"

"There was a key in the cupboard door – with a red ribbon!"

"I didn't notice."

They went out and closed the door. Omri was now feeling desperate.

"We've got to find it. It doesn't work without the key."

They searched the attic till suppertime. Never had

Omri so clearly seen the point of all his mother's urgings to tidy up and keep everything in its proper place. The attic was just a sort of glory-hole, where they could play and leave a total mess, and that was what they always did, only clearing spaces when they needed them for a new layout or for some special game. And their way of clearing was just to shove things aside into ever-more-chaotic heaps.

Underneath the heaps were all the myriad little oddments which were small enough to filter through the bigger things – marbles, wheels of Matchbox cars, bits of Lego, small tools, parachute men, cards, and so on and so on, plus all sorts of fragments which could have been almost anything. At first they just raked through everything. But after a while Omri realized that they would have to clear up systematically. Otherwise it was like the old saying about looking for a needle in a haystack.

He found some boxes and they began sorting things into them – Lego here, parts of games there, water-pistols, tricks and novelties in another. Bigger things they stacked neatly on to what his father rather sarcastically called 'the shelves provided', which normally stood empty since everything was on the floor.

In an amazingly short time the floor was clear except for a few odd things they hadn't found homes for, and a great deal of mud, dust and sand.

"Where did all this come from?" asked Patrick.

"Oh, Gillon brought up boxes of it from the garden to make a desert scene," said Omri. "Months ago. We might as well sweep it up." He looked round. Despite his anxiety about the key, he felt a certain pride. The room looked entirely different – there was real playing-space now.

He went downstairs and fetched a broom, a dustpan and a soft brush.

"We'll have to do this carefully," he said. "It'd be terrible if we threw it away with the sand."

"We could sieve it," suggested Patrick.

"That's a good idea! In the garden."

They carried the sand out in a cardboard box and Omri borrowed his father's large garden sieve. Omri held it and Patrick spooned in the sand and earth with a trowel. Several small treasures came to light, including a ten pence piece. But no key.

Omri was in despair. He and Patrick sat down on the lawn under a tree and he took the two little men out of his pocket.

"Where woman?" Little Bull asked instantly.

"Never mind the wimmin, whur's the vittles?" asked the every-hungry Boone grumpily.

Omri and Patrick fed them some more Toffo, and, with a deep sense of misery, Omri produced the plastic Indian woman from his pocket. Little Bull stopped chewing chocolate crumbs the moment he saw her and gazed in rapture. It was obvious he was half in love with her already. He reached out a hand and tenderly touched her plastic hair.

"Make real! Now!" he breathed.

"I can't," said Omri.

"Why can't?" asked Little Bull sharply.

"The magic's gone."

Now Boone stopped eating too, and he and Little Bull exchanged a frightened look.

"Ya mean – ya cain't send us back?" asked Boone in an awe-stricken whisper. "Never? We got to live in a giants' world for *ever*?"

It was clear that Little Bull had been explaining matters.

"Don't you like being with us?" asked Patrick.

"Wal… Ah wouldn't want to hurt yer feelin's none," said Boone. "But jest think how you'd feel if Ah wuz as big to you as you are to me!"

"Little Bull?" asked Omri.

Little Bull dragged his eyes away from the plastic figure and fixed them – like little bright crumbs of black glass – on Omri.

"Omri good," he pronounced at last. "But Little Bull Indian brave – Indian *Chief*. How be brave, how be chief with no other Indians?"

Omri opened his mouth. If he had not lost the key, he might have rashly offered to bring to life an entire tribe of Indians, simply to keep Little Bull contented. Through his mind flashed the knowledge of what this meant. It wasn't the fun, the novelty, the magic that mattered any more. What mattered was that Little Bull should be happy. For that, he would take on almost anything.

They all sat quietly on the lawn. There seemed nothing more to say.

A movement near the back of the house caught Omri's eye. It was his mother, coming out to hang up some wet clothes. He thought she moved as if she were tired and fed up. She stood for a moment on the back balcony, looking at the sky. Then she sighed and began pegging the clothes to the line.

On impulse Omri got up and went over to her.

"You – you haven't found anything of mine, have you?" he asked.

"No – I don't think so. What have you lost?"

But Omri was too ashamed to admit he'd lost the key she'd told him to be so careful of. "Oh, nothing much," he said.

He went back to Patrick, who was showing the men an ant. Boone was trying to pat its head like a dog, but it wasn't very responsive.

"Well," Omri said, "we might as well make the best of things. Why not bring the horses out and give the fellows a ride?"

This cheered everyone up and Omri ran up and brought the two ponies down carefully in an empty box. Next Patrick stamped a small patch of the lawn hard to give the horses a really good gallop. Quite a large black beetle alighted on the flattened part, and Little Bull shot it dead with an arrow. This cheered him up a bit more (though not much). While the ponies grazed the fresh grass, he kept giving great love-sick sighs and Omri knew he was thinking of the woman.

"Maybe you'd rather not stay the night now," Omri said to Patrick.

"I want to," said Patrick. "If you don't mind."

Omri felt too upset to care one way or the other. When they were called in to supper he noticed that Adiel was trying to be friendly, but he wouldn't speak to him. Afterwards Adiel took him aside.

"What's up with you now? I'm trying to be nice. You got your silly old cupboard back."

"It's no good without the key."

"Well, I'm sorry! It must have dropped out on the way up to the attic."

On the way *up* to the attic! Omri hadn't thought of that.

"Will you help me find it?" he asked eagerly. "Please! It's terribly important!"

"Oh… all right then."

The four of them hunted for half an hour. They didn't find it.

After that, Gillon and Adiel had to go out to some function at school, so Patrick and Omri had the television to themselves. They took out the two men and explained this new magic, and then they all watched together. First came a film about animals, which absolutely transfixed both the little men. Then a Western came on. Omri thought they ought to switch off, but Boone, in particular, set up such a hullabaloo that eventually Omri said, "Oh – all right. Just for ten minutes, then."

Little Bull was seated cross-legged on Omri's knee, while Boone, who had somehow gravitated back to Patrick, preferred to stand in his breast-pocket, leaning his elbows along the pocket top with his hat on the back of his head, chewing a lump of tobacco he had had on him. Patrick, who'd heard something of cowboys' habits, said, "Don't you dare spit! There are no spittoons here, you know."

"Lemme listen to 'em talkin', willya?" said Boone. "Ah jest cain't git over how they *talk*!"

Before the ten minutes was up, the Indians in the film started getting the worst of it. It was the usual sequence in which the pioneers' wagons are drawn into a circle and the Indians are galloping round uttering savage whoops while the outnumbered men of the wagon train fire muzzle-loading guns at them through the wagon wheels. Omri could sense Little Bull was getting restive and tense. As brave after brave bit the dust, he suddenly leapt to his feet.

"No good pictures!" he shouted.

"Watcha talkin' about, Injun?" Boone yelled tauntingly across the chasm dividing him from Little Bull. "That's how it was! Mah maw and paw wuz in a fight like thet'n – mah paw tole me he done shot near'nuff fifteen–twenny of them dirty savages!"

"White men move on to land! Use water! Kill game!"

"So what? Let the best man win! And we won! Yippee!" he added as another television Indian went down with his horse on top of him.

Omri was looking at the screen when it happened. In a lull on the soundtrack he heard a thin faint whistling sound, and heard Boone grunt. He looked back at Boone swiftly, and his blood froze. The cowboy had an arrow sticking out of his chest.

For a couple of seconds he remained upright in Patrick's breast pocket. Then, quite slowly, he fell forward.

Omri had often marvelled at the way people in films, particularly girls and women, were given to letting out loud screams at dramatic or awful moments. Now he felt one rise in his own throat, and would have let it out only that Little Bull cried out first.

Patrick, who had not noticed anything amiss till now, looked at Little Bull, saw where his bow-arm was still pointing, and looked down at his own pocket. Over the top of it Boone hung, head down, as limp as a piece of knotted string.

"Boone! Boone!"

"No!" snapped Omri. "Don't touch him!"

Ignoring Little Bull, who tumbled down his trouser-leg to the floor as he moved, Omri very carefully lifted Boone clear between finger and thumb, and laid him across the palm of his hand. The cowboy lay face up with the arrow still sticking out of his chest.

"Is he – dead?" whispered Patrick in horror.

"I don't know."

"Shouldn't we take the arrow out?"

"We can't. Little Bull must."

With infinite care and slowness, Omri laid his hand on the carpet. Boone lay perfectly still. With such a tiny body it was impossible to be sure whether the arrow was stuck in where his heart was, or a little higher up towards his shoulder – the arrow-shaft was so fine you could only make it out by the minute cluster of feathers.

"Little Bull. Come here."

Omri's voice was steely, a voice Mr Johnson himself might have envied – it commanded obedience.

Little Bull, scrambling to his feet after his fall, walked unsteadily to Omri's hand.

"Get up there and see if you've killed him."

Without a word, Little Bull climbed on to the edge of Omri's hand and knelt down beside the prostrate Boone. He laid his ear against his chest just below the arrow. He listened, then straightened up, but without looking at either of the boys.

"Not killed," he said sullenly.

Omri felt his breath go out in relief.

"Take the arrow out. Carefully. If he dies now, it'll be doubly your fault."

Little Bull put one hand on Boone's chest with his fingers on either side of the arrow, and with the other took hold of the shaft where it went into Boone's body.

"Blood come. Need stop up hole."

Omri's mother kept boxes of tissues in every room, mainly so nobody would have an excuse to sit sniffing. Patrick jumped up and took one, tearing off a tiny corner and rolling it into a wad no bigger than a pinhead.

"Now it's got germs on it from your hand," said Omri.

"Where's the disinfectant?"

"In the bathroom cupboard. Don't let my mum see you!"

While Patrick was gone, Omri sat motionless and silent, his eyes fixed on Little Bull, still poised to pull out the arrow.

After a very long minute, the Indian muttered something. Omri bent his head low. "What?"

"Little Bull sorry."

Omri straightened up, his heart cold and untouched.

"You'll be a lot sorrier if you don't save him," was all he said.

Patrick raced back with the bottle of Listerine. He poured a drop into the lid and dipped the little ball of tissue into it. Then he held the cap close to Little Bull.

"Go on," Omri ordered. "Pull it out."

Little Bull seemed to brace himself. Then he began to tremble.

"Little Bull not do. Little Bull not doctor. Get doctor back. He know make wound good."

"We can't," said Omri shortly. "The magic's gone. You must do it. Do it now. Now, Little Bull!"

Again the Indian stiffened, closing his hand tightly around the arrow. Slowly and steadily he drew it out, and threw it aside. Then, as the blood welled out over Boone's check shirt, Little Bull swiftly squeezed the liquid out of the ball of tissue and pressed it against the wound.

"Use your knife now. Cut the dirty shirt away."

Without hesitating, Little Bull obeyed. Boone lay still. His face under its tan had turned ashy grey.

"We need a bandage," said Patrick.

"There's nothing we could use, and we can't move him to wrap it round him. We'll have to use a tiny bit of sticking plaster."

Again Patrick went to the bathroom. Again Omri, Little Bull and Boone were left alone. Little Bull knelt now with his hands loose on his thighs, his head down. His shoulders rose and fell once. Was he sobbing? With shame, or fear? Or – could it be – sorrow?

Patrick returned with the box of Band Aid and a pair of nail scissors. He cut out a square big enough to cover the whole of Boone's chest, and Little Bull stuck it on with great care and even, Omri thought, tenderness.

"Now," said Omri, "take off your Chief's cloak and cover him up warmly."

This, too, Little Bull did uncomplainingly.

"We'll take him upstairs and put him to bed," said Omri. "Oh, God, I wish we had that key and I could get that doctor back!"

As they walked slowly upstairs, he told Patrick about the First World War soldier he had brought to life to tend Little Bull's leg-wound.

"We've got to find that key!" said Patrick. "We've just got to!"

Little Bull, still at Boone's side on Omri's hand, said nothing.

In Omri's room, Patrick made a bed for the cowboy from a folded handkerchief and another woollen square cut from Omri's sweater. Omri slipped a bit of thin stiff card between Boone and his own hand and on this, he transferred the wounded man without too much disturbance which might have started the bleeding again. He was still unconscious.

Little Bull silently stood by. Suddenly he moved. Reaching up, he snatched off his Chief's headdress and threw it violently on to the ground. Before Omri could stop him, he began jumping on it, and in a second or two all the beautiful tall turkey-feathers were bent and broken.

Leaving it lying there, Little Bull took off across the carpet, running as hard as he could over the deep woollen tufts, stumbling sometimes but running always in the direction of the seed-tray and his home. Patrick moved, but Omri said quietly, "Let him alone."

Chapter Fifteen

UNDERFLOOR ADVENTURE

OMRI AND PATRICK decided they must take it in turns to sit up all night with Boone. This was going to be tricky because of light showing under the door, but Omri unearthed the lumpy remains of a candle he had made himself from a candle-making kit.

"We can put it behind the dressing-up crate. Then the light won't show."

They got into their pyjamas. Patrick was supposed to be sleeping on a folding-bed, so they got it ready to avoid arousing suspicion.

When Omri's mother came in to kiss them goodnight, they were both in bed, apparently reading. The fact that Omri was reading in semi-darkness was nothing unusual, she was always on at him about it.

"Oh Omri! Why *won't* you switch your bedside light on? You'll ruin your eyes."

"It doesn't work," said Omri promptly.

"Yes it does. Daddy fixed it this morning. You know what was wrong with it?"

"What?" asked Omri impatiently, wishing, for once, that she would go.

"That wretched rat of Gillon's had made a nest under the floorboards and lined it with bits of insulation it gnawed off the wires. It's a wonder it didn't electrocute itself."

Omri sat up sharply.

"Do you mean it's got loose?"

His mother gave a lopsided smile. "Where have you been keeping yourself? It's been loose since last night — haven't you noticed Gillon frantically looking for it? It seems to have taken up residence under your bed."

"Under my bed!" Omri yelled, leaping out of it and dropping to his knees.

"It's no use looking for it. I mean right under — the floor. Daddy caught a glimpse of it today when he had the boards up, but he couldn't catch it, of course. It's a matter of waiting till it comes out for food, and then—"

But Omri wasn't listening. A rat! That was all they needed.

"Mum, we've got to get it! We've got to!"

"Why? You're not scared of it, are you?"

"Me – scared of that stupid rat? Of course not! But we've got to catch it!" said Omri, feebly yet desperately. "It might run across my face—" He felt wild and furious. How could Gillon have let the thing go? The perils that a rat presented to his little men simply turned his blood cold. And why, of all rooms in the house, should it have chosen his?

He was tearing frantically at the edge of the carpet, trying to pull it back, when his mother hiked him to his feet.

"Omri, that carpet and those floorboards have been taken up once today, they've been put back once and everything tidied up. Rat or no rat, I'm not going through it all again tonight. Now get into bed and go to sleep."

"But—"

"*Into bed*, I said. Now!"

When she used that tone, there was no arguing with her. Omri got into bed, was kissed, and watched the light go off and the door close. As soon as her footsteps had faded, he leapt up again and so did Patrick.

"Now we must definitely stay awake all night. We mustn't close our eyes for a moment," said Omri.

He was hunting through his ancient collection of book-matches for one out of which his father had *not* cut the matches. At last he found one, and lit the candle. They very gently moved Boone's bed out of hiding on to the bedside table, set the candle beside it, and sat one on each side, watching Boone's dreadfully ill-looking face. The pink square of sticking plaster moved fractionally up and down as he breathed – you could hardly see it. It was like watching the long hand of a clock moving – only the strongest concentration enabled them to detect the faint motion.

"Hadn't we better move the seed-tray up here too?" whispered Patrick.

In the moment when Little Bull had shot Boone, Omri had almost been angry enough to have fed him to the rat; but now, his fury had cooled. He certainly didn't want anything awful to happen to him.

"Yes, let's."

Between them they cleared a place on the table and lifted the seed-tray, with its longhouse, fireplace and hitching posts, up out of reach of prowling rodents.

"Careful. Don't frighten the ponies."

The ponies, however, were getting used to being carried about, and hardly looked up from munching the little piles of grass-cuttings. There was no sign of life from the longhouse.

There followed a timeless period of just sitting there silently, their eyes fixed on Boone's still figure in the flickering candlelight. Omri began to feel light-headed after a bit: the candle flame went fuzzy and Boone's body seemed to vibrate as he stared at it. At the very back of his mind, something else was nagging, nagging... He didn't ask himself what this was, because he had a superstitious feeling that if he let his mind wander from Boone, even for a minute, Boone would slip away into death. It was as if only Omri's will – and Patrick's – were keeping that tiny, fragile heart beating.

Suddenly, though, a thought – like a landscape lit up by lightning – flashed to the forefront of Omri's brain. He sat up, his eyes wide open and his breath held.

"Patrick!"

Patrick jumped. He'd been half asleep.

"What?"

"The key! I know where it is!"

"Where? Where?"

"*Right under my feet*. It must have dropped through the floorboards when Dad opened them. There's nowhere else it could be."

Patrick gazed at him in admiration, but also in dismay.

"How are we going to get it?" he whispered.

"We'll have to take up the carpet first. Maybe Dad didn't nail all the boards down."

Moving very quietly, they managed to lift one corner of Omri's bed and kick back the edge of carpet from underneath. Another bit was under the bedside table leg, and that was tricky, but they shifted it between them in the end. Carefully they folded the corner of carpet back on itself, exposing the boards. Omri then stuck his fingers down the narrow crack at the ends of the boards, one after another, testing to see if they could be lifted. Only one of them could. The rest were nailed down to the joists underneath.

Making as little noise as possible — he hadn't heard his parents go to bed yet — Omri prised up the short end of board. A hole, about the size of a man's foot, gaped in the light of the candle Patrick was holding. Even when he put the candle down the hole, they couldn't see much.

"We'll have to risk the bedside light," Omri said.

They switched it on, and carried it on its flex down to the hole. Kneeling on the floor, they peered into the depths. They could make out the dusty lath-and-plaster several centimetres down — the topside of the ceiling of the room below. The room where Omri's parents were now sitting...

"We'll have to be dead quiet or they'll hear us."

"Dead quiet doing what?" asked Patrick. "It's not there. You'd see it if it was."

"It must be under one of the nailed-down boards," said Omri despairingly.

At that moment they heard Little Bull calling them, and they stood up.

He was standing outside the longhouse, naked but for his breech-cloth. His hair hung loose, his face and chest and arms were smeared with ashes, his feet were bare.

"Little Bull! What are you doing?" asked Omri, aghast at his appearance.

"Want fire. Want make dance. Call spirits. Make Boone live."

Omri looked at him for a moment and felt an ache in his throat that reminded him painfully of his babyish days, when he used to cry so much – days he thought he had left behind forever.

"Little Bull, dancing won't do any good. The spirits won't help. We need a doctor. To get the doctor we need the key. Would you help find it?"

Little Bull didn't move a muscle. "I help."

Gently Omri picked him up. He knelt on the floor and put his hand down in the hole. Patrick held the light. Omri opened his hand and Little Bull stood on it, looking around into the dusty dark tunnel stretching away under the floor.

"I think it's somewhere down there," Omri said quietly, "on the other side of that wooden wall. You'll have to find a way through, a hole or crack or something. We'll give you all the light we can, but it's bound to be awfully dark on the other side. Do you think you can do it?"

"I go," said Little Bull immediately.

"Right. Start looking for a way through."

Little Bull, a tiny, vulnerable figure, strode off through the dust into the darkness under the floor.

Omri pulled the lampshade off the bedside lamp and thrust the bulb down into the hole. He couldn't get his head in to watch, and Little Bull went out of sight almost at once.

"Is there a way through?" he whispered down the tunnel.

"Yes," came Little Bull's voice. "Big hole. I go through. Omri give light."

Omri pushed the light down as far as he could, but the base of the lamp made it stick.

"Can you see anything?" he whispered as loudly as he dared.

There was no answer. He and Patrick knelt there for an age. There wasn't a sound. Then Patrick said suddenly, "Did he take his bow and arrows?"

"No. Why?"

"What if – Omri – what if he meets the rat?"

Omri had totally forgotten about the rat in the excitement of realizing what had happened to the key. Now he felt a strange jerk in his chest, as if his heart had hiccupped.

He bent his head till his face was in the hole. He could smell the dust. The bright bulb was between him and the place where Little Bull had presumably gone through a hole in the joist into the next section of the under-floor space. A hole! What could make a hole right through a joist? What else but a rat, gnawing away all day? A rat at this moment out on his night-prowl, a hungry rat who hadn't eaten for twenty-four hours – a pink-eyed, needle-toothed, omniverous, giant rat?

"Little Bull!" called Omri frantically into the blankness. "Come back! Come back!"

Utter silence. And then he heard something. But it wasn't Little Bull's voice. It was the scuttering sound of a rodent's hard little hairless feet on lath-and-plaster.

"*Little Bull!*"

"Omri!" It was a voice from the room below. "What are you doing up there?"

It was his mother. Then, quite distinctly, he heard his father's voice. "I can hear that blasted rat pattering about overhead. It's probably keeping the boys awake."

"I'd better go up," said his mother. A door closed below and they heard her coming up the stairs. Even this dire prospect hardly had power to do more than push Omri's desperation one stage further. He probably wouldn't have moved from his place on the floor if Patrick hadn't acted swiftly.

"Quick! Light off! Into bed!"

He pulled Omri up, snatched the lamp out of his hand and switched it off. The candle was still down the hole. Patrick shoved the floorboard roughly back into position and moved the carpet so that it more or less covered the boards if you didn't look closely. Then he pushed Omri into his bed, covered him up – the footsteps were nearly at the door – and had just flung himself down on the folding bed when the door opened.

Omri lay there with his eyes squeezed shut thinking, "Don't put the light on! Don't put the light on!" Light was coming into the room from the landing, but not enough to see anything much. His mother stood there for what seemed a hundred years. Finally she whispered, "Are you boys asleep?" Needless to say, she got no reply. "Omri?" she tried once more. Then, after another hundred years, during which Omri imagined Little Bull bitten in half by the rat right underneath where he was lying, the door closed again, leaving them in darkness.

"Wait – wait—" breathed Patrick.

It was torture to wait. The rat had stopped moving when all the scuffling and footsteps had started, that was something; but now it was quiet again, Omri imagined it creeping towards its prey, its pink nose twitching, its albino whiskers trembling hungrily… Oh, how, *how* could he have let Little Bull go down there? Boone's death would at least not have been his fault, but if Little Bull was killed Omri knew he would never forgive himself.

At long, long last the living-room door closed and both boys stole out of bed again. Patrick reached the light first. Omri grabbed it, but Patrick insisted on looking first to see if Boone was still breathing. He was… They rolled back the carpet and lifted the board again, terrified that each movement would attract the grown-ups below. The home-made candle was burning away in the gloom, like a little torch in a disused mine, throwing its eerie light down the tunnel.

Omri lay down flat. He didn't raise his voice, but he called softly: "Little Bull! Are you there? Come back! You're in terrible danger!"

Silence.

"Oh God! Why doesn't he come?" Omri whispered frenziedly.

At that moment they did hear something. It was hard to identify the sound – it was the rat all right, but what was it doing? There was no running sound, just a sort of tiny shock, as if it had made one short, sudden movement.

A pounce?

Omri's heart was in his mouth. Then there were other sounds. If he had not got used to straining his ears to catch the voices of the little men, he might not have heard it. But he did hear it, and hope nearly lifted him off the ground. It was a faint, light scrambling sound, the sound of a small body getting through a hole in a hell of a hurry.

Omri pulled the lamp back out of the hole and thrust his arm in instead, his hand open. Almost at once, he felt Little Bull run into it. Omri closed his fingers, just as something warm and furry brushed against their backs. He snatched his arm out, grazing his knuckles against the splintery wood.

There was something else in his hands — something cold and knobbly, twice as heavy as Little Bull. He opened his fingers, and both boys leant over to look.

Sitting on Omri's palm, filthy and bedraggled but triumphant, was Little Bull, and cradled in his arms, trailing cobwebs and a red satin ribbon, was the missing key.

"You've done it! Oh, Little Bull — good for you! Now — quick — Patrick, get the candle up and put the floor back. I'll find the Red-Cross man."

Reckless now, they switched the top light on. Patrick, being as quiet as he could, replaced the floorboard and the carpet, while Omri looked through the figures jumbled up in the biscuit tin. Luckily the figure of the army medical orderly was right on top, still holding his precious doctor's bag. Little Bull, meanwhile, stood beside the pallet-bed on which Boone was lying, staring down at him, still clutching the key in his arms.

Omri took it from him, thrust the plastic man into the cupboard, and turned the key. He made himself count to ten while Patrick watched, pop-eyed and scarcely breathing. Then he opened the door.

There stood his old friend Tommy, his bag at his feet, rubbing his eyes and frowning around him.

His face cleared as he saw Omri.

"Cor! Well! It's you again. I don't half pick my moments to drop off to sleep, I must say! Thundering great Minnie whining over – thought I was a gonner!"

"What's a Minnie?" asked Patrick in a croaky voice.

"What, another of you?" asked Tommy, gaping. "I must've eaten too much cheese for me dinner! Shouldn't give us cheese before a big attack... very hard on the stomach, especially when it's churned up anyway, with nerves. What's a Minnie? It's our name for a *minnenwerfer* – that's one of them big German shells. Make an 'orrible row they do, even before they land, a sort of whistle which gets louder and louder, and then – KERBOOM! Then blokes with my job has to pick themselves up and run as quick as you like to where it fell, if it fell in a trench, to take care of the wounded."

"We've got a wounded man here we want you to take care of," said Omri quickly.

"Oh, yes? The old redskin again, is it?"

"No, it's another one. Could you step on to my hand?"

Omri lifted him to where Boone lay, and Tommy at once knelt down and began a professional examination.

"He's in a bad way," he said after a few moments. "Could do with a blood transfusion really. I'll have to have this plaster off and look at his wound..." He was cutting it off with a minute pair of scissors as he spoke. The anxious watchers saw that the tuft of tissue underneath was now red with blood, but Tommy said, "Bleeding's stopped, that's one good thing. What was it, a bullet?"

"An arrow," said Omri, and Little Bull shivered all over.

"Oh yes — of course — I see that now. Well, I'm not much up on arrow-wounds. Head's not still in there, I hope?"

"No, it was pulled out."

"Good, good. Lucky it missed his heart. Well, I'll see what I can do." He got the hypodermic out of his bag and fiddled with it for a moment, then plunged the needle into Boone's chest. After that he stitched up the wound, put a field-dressing on it, and got Little Bull to help him peel off the rest of the old, blood-stained plaster.

"You a pal of his, are you?" he asked the Indian.

Little Bull stared at him, but did not deny it.

"Then look here. When he wakes up, you keep giving him these here pills. They're iron, see? Build him up. And these as well, they're for the pain. What we have to hope is that there won't be no infection."

"We need penicillin for him," said Patrick, who had once had a bad cut on his foot which had turned septic.

Tommy looked at him blankly. "Penicillin? What's that when it's at home?"

Omri nudged Patrick. "They hadn't invented it in his time," he whispered.

"Best thing I can suggest is a drop of brandy," said Tommy, and, taking out a flask, poured something down Boone's throat. "Look there," he said cheerfully, "he's getting a better colour already. He'll open his eyes soon, I wouldn't wonder. Keep him warm, that's the ticket. Now I must be getting back – waking up, I mean. If that there Minnie's landed, I'll be in demand, and no mistake!"

Omri carried him back to the cupboard.

"Tommy," he said. "What if – what if the Minnie had fallen on *you*?"

"Couldn't a done, could it? If it had've, I wouldn't be having this here dream, would I, I'd be singing with an 'eavenly choir! Cheeribye – cor, hurry up and shut that door, I think I can hear 'em calling 'Stretcher-bearer' already!"

Omri smiled gratefully at him. He hated to send him back, but obviously he wanted to go.

"Goodbye, Tommy – thanks. And good luck!" And he shut the door.

From the other end of the table, Little Bull suddenly called, "Omri come! Boone open eyes! Boone wake up!"

Omri and Patrick turned. Sure enough, there was Boone, staring up into Little Bull's face.

"What happened?" he got out in a faint, shaky voice.

Nobody liked to tell him, but at last Little Bull had to confess.

"Me shoot," he said.

"Watcha talkin' about, ya crazy Injun? Ah asked ya, what happened in the *picture*? Did them settlers beat the redskins and git to whur they wuz aimin' to git to? Or did the redskins carry off the wimmin and scalp all the men, the dirty low-down savages?"

Little Bull drew in his breath. His head, which had been hanging in shame, came up sharply, and to Omri's horror he actually saw his hand go to his belt for his knife. Luckily it wasn't there. But he jumped to his feet.

"Boone shut mouth! Not say bad words, not insult Indian braves, or Little Bull shoot again, this time kill good, take scalp, hang on pole – Boone scalp too dirty hang on belt of Indian Chief!"

And he snatched his Chief's cloak off Boone's body and swirled it proudly back round his own shoulders.

Omri was shocked, but Patrick was laughing so hard he could scarcely hold it in. But he controlled himself enough to wrap Boone up in the cut-out blanket to keep him warm.

Omri snatched Little Bull up between finger and thumb.

"Oh, so you're a Chief again, are you?" he hissed furiously. "Chiefs ought to know how to keep their tempers! Here—" He picked the broken headdress off the floor and fitted it lopsidedly on to Little Bull's black hair. "Now, Chief – have a good look at yourself!" And he held Little Bull up before a mirror. Little Bull took one look, and then hid his face in his hands. "Just you remember what you did – to your friend!"

"Not friend. Enemy," muttered Little Bull. But the anger had gone out of him.

"Whatever he is, you've got a job to do. Where are those pills? You're to see that he gets them. We can't – we can't even see them. So it's up to you! And when Boone is better, do you know what you're going to do? You're going to make him your blood-brother!"

Little Bull shot him a quick, startled look. "Blood-brother?"

"I know all about it," Omri went on. "You both make little cuts on your wrists and tie them together so the blood mingles, and after that you can't be enemies ever again. It's an old Indian custom."

Little Bull looked baffled. "Not Indian custom."

"I'm sure it is! It was in a film I saw."

"White man idea. Not Indian."

"Well, this Indian's going to do it. And you can smoke a peace-pipe. Don't tell me that's not an Indian custom either!"

"Not Iroquois. Other tribes."

"Couldn't you do it, just this once?"

Little Bull was silent for a moment, thinking. Then Omri saw that crafty look that he knew of old coming on to the Indian's face.

"Good," he said. "Little Bull give Boone medicine, make him my brother when strong. And Omri put plass-tick in box, make real wife for Little Bull."

"Not tonight," said Omri firmly. "We've had enough excitement. Tonight you stand guard over Boone, give him his pills when he needs them, drinks of water and all that. Tomorrow, if everything's all right, I'll bring your woman to life. That's a promise."

Chapter Sixteen

BROTHERS

OMRI HAD FULLY intended to go to sleep – Patrick did, almost immediately – but he couldn't, tired though he was.

Instead, he lay in the candle-light, his head turned towards the table where Boone lay, and Little Bull sat cross-legged next to him, erect and watchful. Sometimes Omri would close his eyes, but he did no more than doze; each time he opened them, he would meet Little Bull's unblinking stare.

It was partly the rat which kept him awake. It pattered around under the floor for hours, making Omri nervous, but it never came anywhere near the men. No, that wasn't the main thing. The main thing was Omri's thoughts.

What was he going to do?

He would bring Little Bull's woman to life as he had promised. But then what?

It had been hard enough with only one little being to feed, protect and keep secret. Much harder after Boone came. Now, with the woman, there'd be three. Young as he was, Omri knew that one woman and two men spelt trouble.

For all Little Bull's unpredictable moods, his demands, his occasional cruelties, Omri liked him. He wanted to keep him. But he knew, now, that that was impossible. Whichever way he thought about it, the end was the same – disaster of some kind. Whatever magic had brought this strange adventure about must be put to use again, to send the little people back to their own place and time.

Having decided this, however sadly and reluctantly, Omri's stressful thoughts let go their hold on him. He drifted off to sleep. When he opened his eyes again, dawn was breaking; the morning chorus of birds was just beginning. The candle had burnt itself out. The rat had gone to sleep. So had Little Bull, nodding over his bow... Omri peered closely at Boone. The yellow field-dressing on his wound moved steadily up and down; his skin had lost the grey look. He was better... Of course Little Bull shouldn't have gone to sleep, but just the same, he had done his best. Omri slipped out of bed.

His blazer was hanging from a hook at the back of his door. He took the paper-bag with the woman in it out of the pocket. Moving on tiptoe, he went to the cupboard, took out the plastic soldier, put in the plastic Indian girl, and locked the cupboard door again.

When he heard little movements, he unlocked the cupboard and opened the door a crack, so she wouldn't be frightened in the dark. Then he got back into bed, covered himself up all except his eyes, and stayed perfectly still to watch what would happen.

At first nothing did. Then, slowly, stealthily, the door was pushed a little further open. Out crept a beautiful Indian girl. There was enough light in the room now for Omri to see the black of her hair, the chestnut brown of her skin, the bright red of her dress. He couldn't see her expression, but he guessed she was bewildered. She glanced all round, and at once spotted Boone lying on the ground and Little Bull dozing beside him.

She approached them cautiously. For a few moments she lingered behind Little Bull, clearly not sure whether she should touch and wake him or not. She decided against it, and, circling Boone's feet, sat herself cross-legged on his other side, facing Little Bull.

She sat staring at him. The three of them were so utterly still that they might have been plastic again. Then a blackbird outside gave a particularly loud chirrup and Little Bull sat up sharply.

At once he saw her. His whole body gave a jolt. Omri felt a prickling up the back of his neck. The way they looked at each other! It went on a long time. Then, slowly and both together, they rose to their feet.

Little Bull spoke to her quietly in his strange, rustling language which did not move his lips. She answered. He smiled. Standing there on either side of Boone, not touching, they talked for some minutes in low voices. Then he put out his hand and she put hers into it.

They stood silently. Then their hands dropped. Little Bull pointed at Boone, and began talking again. The girl crouched down, touched Boone gently and expertly. She looked up at Little Bull and nodded. Then Little Bull looked around the room. He saw Omri.

Omri put his finger to his lips and shook his head, as if to say, "Don't tell her about me."

Little Bull nodded. He took the girl by the hand and led her to the seed-tray, up the ramp and into the longhouse. After a moment or two, he came out again. He ran the length of the table till he stood on its edge, as near to Omri as he could get. Omri leant forward so they could talk quietly.

"Do you like her?"

"Fit wife for Chief." Omri realized this was as near to a word of thanks as he was likely to get, but he didn't mind. "Now Omri hear Little Bull. Woman say, Boone good.

Not die. Little Bull pleased. Omri take Boone, put in longhouse. Woman take care, give little medicines—" He held up the pill boxes. "Omri get food. Make wedding feast."

"How can you have a wedding feast with only two Indians?"

"Yes… not good. Omri make more Indian, come to feast?" he asked hopefully. When Omri shook his head, Little Bull's face fell.

"Little Bull, wouldn't you rather have your wedding feast at home with your own tribe?"

Little Bull was no fool. He understood at once. He stood still, staring at Omri.

"Omri put in box. Send back," he said. His voice was very flat – Omri couldn't tell if he liked the idea or not.

"What do you think? Wouldn't it be better?"

Very slowly, the Indian nodded his head. "And Boone?"

"Boone too."

"Make him my brother first."

"Yes. Then I'll send you all back."

"When?"

"When Boone's well enough."

Now that Omri had decided, every day that passed was important because it was one day nearer to the last.

Patrick was as sad as he was, but he didn't argue against Omri's decision.

"It's the only way, really," Patrick said. After that he didn't talk about it any more, he just tried to be at Omri's house as much as possible.

He couldn't do things with Boone much, of course, even though, in a day or two, Boone was sitting up in the longhouse and demanding to talk to his horse (which was brought to the entrance for the purpose) and whining for all sorts of special food. And drink.

"Ah cain't be expected t'git muh strength back if ya won't gimme some o' the hard stuff," he nagged. He even pretended to have a relapse. Omri pinched a nose-dropperful of whisky from his parents' drinks cupboard and squeezed two large drops down Boone's throat before the Indian girl (whose name was Twin Stars, a reference to her bright eyes, Omri supposed) succeeded in conveying the fact that Boone was perfectly all right and that his faint was faked.

Still, after he'd had his drink Boone seemed so much better that Omri and Patrick decided it wouldn't do him any harm ("He's used to it, after all!") and thereafter Boone got a liquor ration three times a day. And did very well on it.

"He'll be ready to go back tomorrow," said Omri on the fourth day, when Boone, having had a leg up from Little Bull, managed to ride his horse round the seedbox at a steady walk. "They'll probably look after him better than we can, in his own time."

A thought struck him, and he fished out of his pocket the drawing Boone had done.

"Boone, is this your home town?"

"Shore is!"

Omri studied it closely under the magnifying glass. Away up the street he saw a little sign reading 'Doctor'.

"Is he a good doctor?"

"'Bout as good as any out West, Ah reckon. Fish a bullet out of a man's arm or cut his foot off fer snake-bite as neat as kin be. I seen him bring a pal o' mine back from the dead, near enough, by puttin' a hot coal in his belly-button. He never operates till a man's dead drunk, *and* he don't charge extry for the likker neither!"

Omri and Patrick looked at each other. "You'd feel that you were in good hands, with this – er – doctor looking after you?" Patrick asked worriedly.

"Shore would! Anyhow, don't need no sawbones now, m'wound's healin' up fine. S'long as Ah git mah whisky, Ah'll be as good as new."

Boone bore not the slightest ill-will towards Little Bull for having shot him.

"That there's a Injun's natural nature. Pore simple critter c'd no more help himself than Ah kin keep away from muh horse and muh bottle!"

The night before Omri had decided to send them back,

they held the blood-brotherhood ceremony.

"I wish we could ask *our* brothers!" said Patrick to Omri at school that day. "Supposing we tell them one day about this — they'll never believe us."

"Sending them back," said Omri slowly, "doesn't mean the magic won't work any more. I'm going to put the key away somewhere so I won't be tempted; but it will always be there."

Patrick looked at him wonderingly. "I never thought of that," he said slowly. "So there'd be nothing to stop us — months or even years from now — from bringing Boone and Little Bull back again. To visit."

"I don't know," said Omri. "Maybe their time is different from ours. It would be awful if they were old, or—" But he couldn't say "or dead". Both Boone and Little Bull came from such dangerous times. Omri shivered and changed the subject.

"As for our brothers coming," he said, "all I want of my brothers is to keep that rat in its cage." The rat had been caught by Omri after a long, patient wait with cheese and a fishing-net, and Omri had threatened Gillon with the worst fate imaginable if he let it get away again.

The two boys went to Yapp's after school and bought feast-food for the ceremony — salted nuts, crisps, Hula Hoops and chocolate. Omri bought a quarter of a pound of best mince at the butcher's for tiny hamburgers (a teaspoonful would have been enough, but the butcher wasn't interested in that). They got bread, biscuits, cake and Coke from Omri's mother, and Omri sneaked another dropperful of 'the hard stuff', without which Boone would certainly not consider it a festive occasion at all.

Omri was rather surprised Boone had agreed to be blood-brother to a 'stinkin' redskin' at all, but he actually seemed rather to fancy the idea.

"T'ain't jest anyone gits ter be blood-brother to an Injun chief, y'know," he said proudly, as he rolled up his sleeve and Twin Stars carefully swabbed his arm with soap and water. But when he saw Little Bull sharpening his knife on a pebble he turned pale.

"Hell! It'll hurt!" he muttered, but Patrick told him not to be a coward.

"It's only a nick, it's nothing at all!"

"Easy fer you!" retorted Boone. "I ain't sure this is sich a nice idee, after all…"

But he cheered up when he saw the campfire being kindled, and smelt the meat Twin Stars was cooking on a pointed stick; and when Omri gave him a good swig from the dropper he swaggered up to Little Bull and offered his arm with a drunken flourish.

"Chop away, brother!" he said loudly.

Little Bull went through a whole routine first, cleaning himself, offering up loud chanting prayers to the spirits and performing a marvellous stamping dance round the fire. Then he nicked his own wrist with the point of his knife. The blood welled up. Boone took one look and burst into tears.

"Ah don't wanna! Ah changed m'mind!" he bawled. But it was too late for that. Little Bull seized his arm, and before Boone knew what was happening the deed was done.

Twin Stars bound their wrists together with a strip of hide torn from the hem of her red dress. Boone looked at it in a bemused way and said, "Gee whiz. We done it! I'm part-Injun! Wal... Ah guess Ah cain't say nothin' 'gainst 'em in the future."

Then the two 'brothers' sat on the ground. Little Bull took out a short-stemmed pipe and some rather evil-smelling tobacco, and he and Boone took it in turns to puff at it. Twin Stars served them the cooked meat, and all the rest of the feast. Patrick and Omri offered their congratulations and tucked into their own food. They kept the campfire going with tiny bits of broken matchsticks and a bit of coal-dust Omri had collected from the outside bunker, which, when sprinkled on the flame, made it spit minute sparks. Looking at it, and the three little figures round it, the boys gradually lost their sense of size altogether.

"I feel as if I were the same as them," murmured Patrick.

"Me too," said Omri.

"I wish we *were* all the same size, then there'd be no problem."

"Don't be funny! No problems, with two full-grown Indians and a crying cowboy?"

"I meant, if we were small. If we could enter their world – sleep in the longhouse – ride the ponies—"

"I wouldn't mind eating one of those hamburgers," said Omri.

Twin Stars was now crouched by the fire, tending it, singing softly. One of the horses whinnied. Boone seemed to have dropped off to sleep, leaning on Little Bull's shoulder. Little Bull alone was aware of the boys, watching them. He beckoned to Omri with his free hand.

When Omri bent to hear him, he said, "Now!"

"Now? You mean, to go back?"

"Good time. All happy. Not wait for morning."

Omri looked at Patrick. He nodded slowly.

"When you go into the cupboard," Omri said, "you must hold Twin Stars. Or she may not go back with you."

"Woman go back with Little Bull. Little Bull hold, not let go. And horse! Little Bull only Iroquois with horse!"

"But Boone must go separately. Don't drag him back to your time, your people would kill him even if you are his new brother."

Little Bull looked at Boone, asleep at his side, and at their joined wrists. Then he took his knife and cut the thong that bound them together. Patrick gently lifted Boone up.

"Don't forget his hat! He'd never forgive us if we let him leave that behind."

To be safe, they sat Boone on his horse. Cowboys often ride in their sleep, and he didn't stir as Little Bull led him down the ramp, across the table and up another ramp that Omri stood against the rim of the cupboard. Then Little Bull went back to the seed-tray. Carefully he and Twin Stars put out the fire with earth. Little Bull took a last look at his longhouse. Then he put Twin Stars on to his pony's back, and led them after Boone.

They stood all together in the bottom of the cupboard. Nobody spoke. Omri had his hand on the door when Patrick suddenly said, "I'm going to wake Boone up. I don't care, I've got to say goodbye to him!"

Hearing his name, Boone woke up by himself, so suddenly he nearly fell off his horse and had to clutch the high pommel of his saddle.

"Watcha want, kid?" he asked Patrick, whose face was close to him.

"You're going home, Boone. I wanted to say goodbye."

Boone stared at him and then his face slowly crumpled.

"Ah cain't stand sayin' goodbye," he choked out as tears began to stream. He pulled a huge grubby handkerchief from his pocket. "Ah jest re-fuse t'say it, that's all! Ah'll only bust out cryin' if Ah do." And he blew a trumpet-blast on his nose.

Omri and Little Bull were staring at each other. Something else was needed – some special farewell. It was Little Bull who thought of it.

"Omri give hand!"

Omri put his hand forward. The pony braced his legs but Little Bull held him steady. He took hold of Omri's little finger, drew his knife and pricked it in the soft part. A drop of blood appeared. Then Little Bull solemnly pressed his own right wrist against the place and held it there.

"Brother," he said, looking up at Omri with his fierce black eyes for the last time.

Omri withdrew his hand. Little Bull jumped on to the back of his pony behind Twin Stars, holding her round the waist so that he, she and the pony made one unit which could not be separated during whatever kind of unearthly journey they had to make together through the unknown regions of time, space – proportion.

Little Bull raised his arm in the Indian salute.

Omri put his hand on the door. He could hardly bear to do it. He had to set his teeth. Boone and his horse stood patiently, but the Indian's pony started to prance and sidle. It put up its head and gave a long challenging neigh.

"Now!" cried Little Bull.

Omri drew in his breath, closed the door and turned the key.

He and Patrick stood frozen with the sadness, the strangeness of it. The magic was working at this moment… Both of them silently counted ten. Then, very slowly, Omri, whose hand had not left the key, turned it back again and swung open the door.

There they were, the two plastic groups – forms, outlines, shells of the real, real creatures they had been. Each boy lifted out his own and helplessly examined it. The life-giving details were blurred – plastic can't show fine beadwork, the perfection of hair and muscle, the folds of cloth, the sheen of a pony's coat or the beauty of a girl's skin. The figures were there, but the people, the personalities, were gone.

Patrick's eyes met Omri's. Both were wet.

"We could bring them back. Just as quick," he said huskily.

"No."

"No… I know. They're home by now."

Omri put his group, the Indian, the girl and the pony, on the shelf nearest his bed where he could see it easily. Patrick slipped the mounted cowboy into his pocket, cupping his hand round it almost as if to keep it warm.

Then Omri took the key and left the room.

His mother was in the kitchen getting everyone a hot drink before bed. She took one look at Omri's face and her hands became still.

"What's happened? What's wrong?"

"Nothing. Mum, I want you to keep this key. I lost it. Lucky I found it again, but you told me it was important... Better if you keep it. Please."

She nearly refused, but then, looking at him, she changed her mind and took the key from him.

"I'll get a chain and wear it," she said, "like I always meant to."

"*You* won't lose it, will you?"

She shook her head, and suddenly reached for him and hugged his face against her. He was shaking. He broke away and ran back to his room, where Patrick was still standing with his hand in his pocket gazing at the cupboard.

"Come on, I'm going to put all sorts of medicines in it," Omri said loudly. "Bottles of pills and stuff Mum's finished with. We'll pretend it's a doctor's drug-cupboard, and we can mix lots of them together..."

His voice petered out. Those were silly games, such as he had played – before. He didn't feel the slightest interest in them now.

"I'd rather go for a walk," said Patrick.

"But what shall I do with the cupboard?" asked Omri desperately.

"Leave it empty," said Patrick. "In case."

He didn't say in case what. But he didn't have to. Just to know you *could*. That was enough.

Postscript

This novel was originally written in the late 1970s when my sons were still children. We had come back from Israel, where all the boys were born and where we lived in a kibbutz. Now we were living in London in quite a big house and we were having a struggle keeping it all together. I was pretty rattled a lot of the time because I had to keep writing books while trying to run a home. An American friend of mine told me, "You're a pioneer – yours is the first generation of middle-class women that has had to manage homes and families without servants and earn a living at the same time. Your mother didn't work after she got married; and *her* mother didn't work *and* had servants."

Whether I can dignify my frequent feeling of being out of my depth by calling it "pioneering" I don't know, but despite my wonderful husband's help, it was very hard, and I was always looking feverishly for ideas. Some of my best ones came in the spontaneous form of bedtime stories, and, since I was usually busy writing adult novels at that time, I would tell them and forget them.

But once when a publisher asked me to write a children's book, and I was desperate, my youngest son reminded me of a bedtime story I'd told him several years before, about a little bathroom cupboard we found in our first London house that brought plastic toys to life. He'd remembered it so clearly that he was able to help me while I was writing it. So I wrote it very quickly (in only about three months) and I left in it a lot of names – including his, Omri, the hero of the story – and places and things and even animals, that I had originally put in my "telling" story for my son's benefit. Omri's name, from being almost unknown outside Israel, is now quite famous, but I didn't anticipate that at the time.

The cupboard was one of the real things, and I still have it. Unlike a lot of other things in the book, which were based on reality but which I changed for the story, the cupboard is exactly as I described it – a small, shabby, white-painted metal cabinet "with a mirror in the door, the kind you find over the basin in old-fashioned bathrooms". It is now very important to me, as you can imagine. For example, when recently I was in a hotel in Seattle which caught fire and a woman ran past our door screaming at us to leave the hotel immediately, I turned back (as one is forbidden to do) and picked up the cupboard in its carrying bag before running down the back stairs. I carry this cupboard about with me and show it to children when I visit schools. They're often surprised at its plainness. I tell them, "Don't judge a book by its cover and don't judge an object by its surface appearance. This *is* a magic cupboard."

How else to explain how it changed my life, brought me fame, prizes, money, new friends and wonderful travel opportunities? Of course it's magic.

This book, which I had thought was just a book, proved to be the biggest success I'd written since my first novel, *The L-Shaped Room* (which wasn't for children). *The Indian in the Cupboard* changed the tide for us – I mean, for our family finances – and it changed my career. I began writing more and more for children, less and less for grown-ups. Writing for grown-ups is a challenge you shouldn't turn away from, but it's hard when there's a lot of demand and reward for one kind of writing, not to do more and more of that. Children wrote me letters begging for more adventures of Omri and the Indian, so I tried to oblige. I've written five books about them now, and a lot of other children's books as well. I've really enjoyed the life I've had since *The Indian in the Cupboard* came into it.

Of course, it hasn't all been plain sailing. I wrote the original book in a light-hearted vein and I didn't think too much about strict accuracy. I did a little research about the Iroquois, but not nearly as much as I should have. The success of the book in the United States coincided with the rapid development of ethnic consciousness among American Indians and the resentment of some of them about stereotyping by non-Indian writers.

Postscript

Attacks on the books by certain tribal members has caused me a lot of pain, but it has had a good effect. In later books I took more and more trouble to check my facts. For the fifth book in the series, *The Key to the Indian*, I travelled to Canada to talk to some of today's Mohawks (one of the Six Nations of the Iroquois Confederacy) and I think I've made fewer mistakes in this book. As a result of these efforts, I feel that the books have deepened and become more true. That is now one of my criteria of good writing, and the fact that I am writing fantasy doesn't let me off getting the real things right.

LYNNE REID BANKS

September 2000